Dragon Lord

Dragon Lord

Avril Sabine

Cracked Acorn Productions
Australia

Dragon Lord

Published by

Cracked Acorn Productions

PO Box 1365

Gympie, Queensland 4570

Australia

978-1-925131-03-1 (Kindle)

978-1-925617-42-9 (EPUB)

978-1-925131-26-0 (Print)

Genre: Children's Fantasy

Cover design by Caitlyn Petersen

For my oldest son, who told me I needed to write a story with dragons. Here it is, as ordered.

In a world ruled by those who own dragons it is almost impossible to change your station in life. Fen is an orphan with a short life expectancy and no hope for the future. In the process of trying to steal a dragon for his master, Fen's life looks like it's going to become even shorter. He's faced with a difficult decision. Should he risk everything, including his blood boiling in his veins, for the chance of a future or remain with his corrupt master.

*

This story was written by an Australian author using Australian spelling.

Chapter One

Fen huddled under a damp bush. The steady drip of moisture from the leaves trickled down his back. He drew his arms in tight against his ribs and held his clasped hands at his mouth so he could breathe warmth on them. After pulling the grimy woollen cap down to cover his ears he went back to breathing on his hands.

He had brown eyes, a slightly crooked nose and his worn cotton shirt, patched until it had been thrown in the rubbish, did nothing to keep him from shivering. All that kept him in the cold drizzle was the thought of what would happen if he returned to Rhone empty handed. A shiver went through him at that thought, one that had nothing to do with the damp night.

The door Fen watched opened and two men came out with a lantern. The door closed behind them and they sauntered past the front of the windowless stone building, disappearing around the corner. Once the men were out of sight, Fen slowly counted to ten. Exactly as Rhone had told him. Crawling out from under the bush, he tried to straighten. A leg cramp made him buckle and he bit back a gasp. He kneaded the muscle, his forehead pressed against his knee. He closed his eyes and clenched his teeth in an effort to stay quiet. The pain ebbed away. He took a deep breath and warily rose. After a glance around he hurried to the building.

There was very little moonlight, but enough to see more than shadows. Enough to see the door wasn't quite shut. Fen stared at it. He began to chew on his lip, frowning as he tried to decide what to do. The door should be locked. He took a step away from the door. Stopped. His back could almost feel Rhone's walking stick land across it. He had to go forward. As his hand reached to push against the door, Fen reminded himself of one of the other orphans Rhone had taken in. The one who hadn't risen after Rhone had used his walking stick on him. He'd been dumped in the river with no one to care what happened to him.

Fen slipped inside the building, pulled the door shut and glanced around. Lamps hanging from the ceiling gave off a soft glow of light. Fen stared at them. He'd heard of wizard lamps before but had never seen them. They gave off light but no heat and wouldn't burn anything down if they were knocked over.

There was a lot to burn down. Straw was scattered over the floor and on the raised wooden boxes. Some of the boxes had large eggs nestled around a heat stone. Something else Fen had only ever heard of. He stepped forward. Dirt streaked fingers hesitantly reached out to touch the heat stone. He snatched his fingers back at the last second, forcing his mind to the job at hand. At the end of the room was a rock wall with a metal door set in it. This was where Fen needed to go. Rhone had said the place would be fire proof. He'd never heard of stone or metal catching fire, unless magic was involved.

Fen looked around. Nothing but very large eggs. No one was inside. He shrugged. Who knew how servants of wealthy people thought. If he owned this place he'd make sure it was always locked up real good. He moved forward, more confident now he was out of the rain and no longer shivering. The building was warm from all the heat stones. He considered stealing one but knew Rhone'd take it from him.

Rhone warned each kid he took in that they could only stay with him until they were fifteen or sixteen. After that they were on their own. Even though he didn't know his exact age, he recognised the signs. He didn't want to do anything to make Rhone throw him out any sooner. He wasn't ready to strike out on his own. All he had was a couple of coins, but that wouldn't be enough to help him survive.

The metal door swung open easily and Fen stepped into the room. The floor was heated granite and the sudden warmth on Fen's bare feet sent goosebumps up his arms. He rubbed them and moved into the room. There was a scattering of straw on the floor that looked like it had been walked in from the other room, but that was all the flammable material he could see. The room was divided by rock walls and metal doors, which reached to Fen's chest height to create a stable. He moved to the first one, peering inside at the tumble of limbs.

Four grey coloured dragons lay together, their wings tucked in against their bodies and their arms and legs sprawled out like a basket of kittens that had fallen asleep playing. But they were much bigger than a kitten, more like a mid-sized dog.

Grey dragons were just what Rhone wanted. A new hatchling still not come into its colour. Fen started to open the metal door into the dragon enclosure when a sound made him freeze.

"What are you doing in my stable?"

Fen spun around. "You're a girl!" For a moment he'd expected someone older. He could outsmart another kid.

The girl tossed brown hair, tilting her head so she could look down her pointed nose. Blue eyes glared at him, her hands on her hips. "And you're just a boy." She wrinkled her nose. "A filthy one at that. Don't you ever take a bath?"

"What for?" Fen looked confused.

"You didn't answer my question. And who are you?"

"Who are you?" Fen demanded.

"I asked first. Besides, I'm meant to be here and you don't look like any stableboy I've ever seen. At least they bathe once a week."

"It was cold outside, I came in to get warm." Fen put a whine in his voice in the hope the girl would feel sympathetic.

"Sure." The girl drew the word out. "I'm not stupid. There are grey dragons in that pen. Everyone knows you can only steal grey dragons since you can't blood hunt them until they change colour. Even

I know a dragon's useless until it changes colour and can be tracked."

"I'm no thief. I'm an orphan. It's cold out there."

"What's your name, dragon thief?"

Fen started to move away from the dragons. "I'm cold and starving. I haven't eaten since last night." Both comments were true. Rhone believed a hungry boy was more anxious to do his job and return for a feed.

"Take one more step and I'll alert the guards. And don't think I can't. The right word, even whispered, will set off alarms all over the place."

Fen eyed her carefully. She had to want something from him. There had to be a way to use that against her. "Then why haven't you?"

"Because I think we can help each other."

"How?" His eyes narrowed. "And why would you help me?"

"I haven't decided if I will yet. First I need to know your name and then I need to know why you want a dragon."

Fen sighed. Rhone had told him it'd be the easiest night's work he'd done since he'd taken him in. Nothing was ever simple in life.

"I guess I could always give you a name. It's better than calling you boy, or dragon thief, or even scavenger. Now, you don't look much like a Selig. I have a cousin Selig and he's much bigger than you. You're rather scrawny aren't you?"

Fear started to be replaced by annoyance. "Don't you ever shut up?"

"Shh, this is a tough decision." The girl glared at him again.

"Oh, for peace before you talk me to death. It's Fen. My name's Fen."

The girl smiled. "Now, that wasn't too hard, was it? And yes, I can be quiet." She flashed him another smile. "When I get my own way. Now, why do you want the dragon?"

Fen shook his head, muttering 'spoilt brat' under his breath. "My master wants it."

"What for?"

"How the hell would I know? He'd rap me across the head with his walking stick and yell at me to get out of his business."

The girl sighed. "That doesn't sound good. I don't know what'd be worse." She frowned and then suddenly looked at Fen thoughtfully. "What would you swear to be able to take a dragon tonight?"

"Anything."

"A blood oath?"

Fen went pale under his layer of dirt. "Well..." his

mind quickly tried to find a way out of the situation. "We don't have a wizard to do the spell."

"My father has parchment that's been spelled for blood oaths. Will you sign one?"

"What's the oath?"

"You'll protect the dragon from all harm, even to putting your own life in danger."

Chapter Two

Fen closed his eyes. How could he keep such an oath? With a master like Rhone it'd be impossible. For all he knew the dragon would be slaughtered for parts to sell to wizards for spells. Not every wizard questioned where rare items came from.

But what was he to do if he failed to take a dragon to Rhone? There was no way he could survive on the streets yet. If he served Rhone well, he'd give him a knife and a few coins before sending him on his way. He could protect himself with a knife. Being one of Rhone's boys was what protected him now. But if he failed tonight, that'd quickly change. He thought of the blood oath. Surely he could figure out a way around it.

"Have you fallen asleep?"

Fen's eyes snapped open. "I wish."

"Well? What's your answer?"

"What's your name?" Fen demanded.

"What?"

"Your name. If I swear a blood oath, I want to know who holds it."

The girl nodded, took a breath and then said, "Edana Lenita Behira Yileen Renarlo con Crinitie."

"A bloody royal blood. I should have known." They were the only ones who used the word 'con' to add the mother's family name after the father's family name.

"I'm not that royal. At least a thousand people would have to die before I could get anywhere near the throne."

Fen cast about for something to talk about. Something to take her mind off the blood oath. "What's with the stupid name? Your ma must have the lungs of a diver to call you when she wants you."

"It's not stupid. I'll have you know they're all family names. Besides, everyone calls me Edana."

"Too bossy and annoying to be called that. It sounds more like a girl who sits at embroidery all day and doesn't hang out in stables wearing pants and boots," Fen sneered.

"Just 'cause I'm royal doesn't mean I have to wear stupid frills and be bored all day talking about dresses and parties. I like pants and I love dragons."

"You're more of an Ed. I knew an Ed once and he was as annoying as you."

"I am not." She glared at Fen. "What happened to him if you don't know him now?"

"Upset the wrong person and became fish food."

"What do you mean?"

Fen rolled his eyes. "Don't you know anything?"

"Probably more than you. Now quit stalling. Will you take a blood oath?"

Fen sighed. That hadn't worked. Maybe he could disappear while she was gone. "What choice do I have? Go ahead and get the parchment."

"Not so quickly. I'm not having you run off with a dragon the moment I go." Edana pulled a linen handkerchief out of a leather pouch at the side of her belt and held it out to Fen. "Blood tracker."

Fen shuddered at the thought of blood tracker hounds after him. She was smarter than he'd first thought. "I don't have a knife." He looked warily between the handkerchief and Edana.

Edana smiled. "I do." She pulled out the small knife hung in a sheath on the left side of her belt. In the top of the handle, which was wrapped in leather for comfort, was a blue jewel. When Fen looked at the jewel, she said, "It's spelled so it can't be used against me or taken from the knife without a really loud sound going off. Come on. Are you going to make the cut or will I?"

"I'll do it. You'd probably slice too deep or take a finger off or something." Fen took the knife, pulled back his ragged sleeve and slid the sharp blade against the skin of his arm. A thin line of blood welled up amongst the dirt. The knife still clutched in his hand, he took the handkerchief and smeared blood and dirt on it. He then wiped his blood off the knife blade before he handed it back.

"And the handkerchief." Edana held out her hand.

"You'll give it to me when you get back here?"

"It wouldn't matter. I'd have your blood on the oath. I can use that for blood trackers."

"You wouldn't be as careless with an oath."

"I'll think about it. Stop stalling. The guards come and check on things again in about an hour. I don't think they'll be as helpful as I'm being."

"You aren't being helpful. You want something. What is it?"

"You'll have to wait until I come back. You don't want to be caught do you?" Before Fen could answer, Edana snatched the handkerchief and ran through the metal door.

Fen sighed. How had this day gone so wrong? All he'd needed to do was hide in the bushes and wait for the guards to leave so he could steal a grey dragon. Rhone had made sure the dogs that normally patrolled the grounds wouldn't bother him. He didn't know how. It hadn't been his business. As it was, he'd have to come up with a good story for why he'd be returning late. That'd be difficult.

He started to pace, impatient for Edana to return. When he heard footsteps behind him, he turned swiftly. It was Edana. Pulling her cloak off, she dropped it on the floor near the door that led outside. She rubbed her hands together and then looked up to where Fen stood in the doorway that led to the young dragons.

"It's cold out there. Well, let's get this over. I've written on it already. Do you want to read it?" Edana held the parchment out towards Fen.

"Yeah, right, Ed. What would I need with reading?"

"It's Edana, not Ed. And why can't you read?"

"What would it do for me? Can I eat it? Wear it? Will it keep me warm?"

Edana shook her head. "No, but people can't trick you or charge you more than they should if you can read."

"You're the one who called me thief. What makes

you think a thief would pay for things when they can steal them?"

"Fine. You can't read. It says, the oath is between two unnamed parties who hold this parchment while a binding oath is spoken and the party who seals this with their blood at the end will uphold the oath."

"What's the oath?"

"You need to say your full name, and that you'll protect with your life the dragon given to you by, and then say my name. Say you bind the oath with your blood and it'll boil in your veins if you break it." Edana held the parchment towards Fen.

He hesitated a moment before he took it. "I Fenton will protect with my life the dragon given to me by Edana Lenita… Behira Yileen Renarlo con… Crinitie." He closed his eyes a moment and then opened them and looked into Edana's dark blue eyes. "If I break this oath may my blood boil in my veins." A quick glance showed the cut on his arm had congealed. He needed fresh blood for the spell. He held out his hand for the knife.

Fen slipped the knife into the hand that still held the parchment and then brushed his thumb against the blade. He watched the red droplet form on his thumb. It hung a moment before it fell to the parchment beneath it. To Fen it seemed to hang in mid air before it hit the surface and spread. Once again his eyelids closed and he tried to force thoughts of boiling blood from his mind.

"As it was sealed, let it be paid," Edana said.

Fen opened his eyes to stare at her, unable to speak for a moment. He would find a way around this. "As it was sealed, let it be paid," he finally whispered.

Edana nodded, folded the parchment and slid it into her leather pouch. She held out her hand for her knife and her foot tapped as she waited for Fen to wipe it clean on his shirt hem.

"Argh, disgusting," Edana said when Fen put his thumb in his mouth so the blood wouldn't drip on the floor.

"I don't want anyone else getting hold of my blood. Now what about your hanky?"

"We'll see. Come and have a look at the dragon."

Fen followed her to the last pen. Inside were five dragons. Four coloured, one grey. The coloured dragons curled sleepily together, the grey watched them.

"Why him?" Fen asked.

"This is what I need help with. He can't stay here. In two days if he hasn't changed colour they'll kill him for parts. He can't be tracked unless he changes colour. He's no good to them if they can't protect their investment. So they're going to get what they can for him," Edana said.

"What if he changes colour tomorrow?"

"He's three-months-old in two days time. His egg mates changed within the first week."

"Oh," Fen said. There wasn't anything he could say. Most dragons changed colour within the first week. A few more by the end of the first month. It was a rare dragon that changed colour after three months. Some never changed colour and stayed grey their entire life. A blood tracker couldn't track a grey dragon. It was impossible. No Dragon Lord wanted a dragon that a thief would want to steal. Protecting it would be extremely difficult. They lost enough grey hatchlings to thieves each year without wanting to risk dragons they'd spent time and money feeding and training.

"What could I offer you to take him from here and not give him to your master? I want you to raise him yourself."

"What?" Fen wondered if he'd heard Edana right. The first year of raising a dragon wasn't too bad. They didn't grow much. But by the time they were two they towered over an adult. And who was to look after the dragon when Fen was dead? Dragons could live for hundreds of years.

"I want you to hide him," Edana said more slowly.

"You're completely crazy." Fen took a step away from her. "Mad."

"No I'm not. You could do it. I'll help you," Edana said.

"No way. You don't know Rhone. If he found I'd crossed him, he'd kill me." Fen backed further away.

Edana smiled. "If you take the dragon to Rhone the blood oath will kill you. Taking him there will be the opposite of protecting him."

Chapter Three

He stared at her, trying to figure out a way around the oath. She'd worded it too well. There were only two options. Burn the oath or kill Edana. And he didn't think he could kill her no matter how annoying she was. He eyed her pouch.

Edana glanced down at her pouch. "There's no way you can get the oath back. The pouch is spelled against everyone except my family."

"Why you-" Fen lunged for Edana, pushing her to the ground. She tried to roll away but he grabbed a hold of her plait.

"I'll call the guards."

"What does it matter? I'm dead anyway."

"You're not." Edana tried to pull her plait from his hand, the other fending off the hand going for her throat. "I promise. Hear me. Be your own master."

Fen stilled. He kept Edana's plait twisted around

one hand and the other hand pressed against her throat where both her hands kept trying to pull it away. His brown eyes stared unblinking at her. His woollen cap had come off and short black hair stood up in all directions.

"Speak quickly," Fen warned.

"Let me go first." Edana tugged the hand at her throat.

"I haven't got all night."

Edana swallowed hard. "One of our maids was killed recently. She went home on her day off to visit her parents. Her father had been bitten by a swamp dragon and he didn't get it seen to. The poison sent him mad and he killed them all. His son, who worked the swamps with him, his wife and his daughter. All of them. Then the fever became too bad and his heart stopped. There was an aunt. She was visiting friends and came home to blood everywhere. They had to lock her up. Some people say she hasn't stopped screaming. No one'll go near the place. They say with a death like that the spirits won't rest. You could stay there. It's at the edge of the swamp. All their traps and stuff will still be there. I'll give you some money. You'll be fine and the dragon will be safe."

"Except for the spirits." He tightened his grip on her throat when she tried to shake her head.

"I have a potion for that. Father ordered another potion but the wizard couldn't read his writing so he sent the wrong one. I have money you can have. I'll visit and make sure you have everything you need. Anything. Give me some terms and I'll meet them. I can even teach you to read."

"What do I want with reading? I get along without it."

"You get along, but you don't get anywhere. The ones who run things need to know how to read. To truly be your own master you must learn."

"I can't cross Rhone. He'll kill me."

"He won't have to know. Leave the dragon at the house and go back to him. Tell him there was someone in here all night. You waited for them to come out but they didn't. Anything. Just save the dragon for me," Edana pleaded.

"Why? What's so special about him?"

"He touched my mind. He knows he's doomed. It was like a butterfly wing brushing me. He looked at me with his silver eyes and I knew he was begging me for help. No words, just emotions. If he touched your mind you'd do anything to help him too."

"That's a myth. Dragon's can't mind-read or mind-talk. They'd tell us off for the way we treat them if they could. They have to be plain stupid not to rebel against us for keeping them like slaves. They're animals. Like a horse or dog."

"I'll show you. Let me up and I'll show you."

Fen's eyes narrowed. "I let you up. You show me. If the dragon can't do what you say then you give me the blood oath and let me walk out of here with him. If he does what you say then I take him to your spirit house."

"Deal," Edana said. "But you have to give him time. Ten minutes at least. He's only a baby."

Fen nodded once. His hands let her go and he stood. He picked up his woollen cap, hit it against his leg to remove the straw and pulled it back on. He watched Edana take the grey dragon from the pen and struggle over to him with it. She placed the dragon on the ground in front of him.

"Please touch his mind. Like you did to me. He won't save you unless you do. Please. You asked me to save you. This is all I can come up with. I sat with you every night the past week trying to think of something. And every minute during the day when I can escape my tutors. This is it." Edana stroked the dragon's head. The scales smooth, the ridge down the centre of his head rough. Edana's eyes glittered in the lamplight. "I know he's not much to look at, a bit scrawny, but he's all I can find."

"I haven't got all night," Fen said sharply, annoyed by her last comment.

"You gave him ten minutes. They're not up yet." Edana turned back to the dragon who watched her solemnly. That was all he did. He watched and listened. There were no butterfly touches. Even when Edana made Fen kneel beside the dragon and touch him and look him in the eye. Nothing. Exactly what Fen had expected.

"It's well past your ten minutes." Fen guessed it must be by the frantic tone in Edana's voice. "I told you dragons are just another animal. Come on, Eddie. Give up. Let me have my oath back. You made a deal. And the hanky."

Edana shoved the parchment and handkerchief at him. "You're cruel and heartless. I hope you rot in hell."

She turned away as Fen bent to pick up the dragon before he moved into the next room. He let the metal door close softly behind him and put the dragon down on one of the raised areas. Even though there were no eggs here, there was still a heat stone. He stared wistfully at it and then at the door to outside.

He shoved his blood oath and the handkerchief into the pouch that hung at his rope belt and looked around for something to wrap the dragon in. He couldn't walk the streets with his arms filled by a dragon. People would notice. Seeing folded blankets in a corner he grabbed one. It was soft and thick so he picked up another. It'd keep the damp off him until he reached Rhone's place. Then Rhone would probably take it from him.

"Rich people," Fen muttered as he tied the blanket at his neck so it draped like a cloak. "These are too good for animal blankets." He took the other blanket to the dragon. As he was about to wrap him he felt something. Like butterfly wings against his mind.

"I imagined it." Fen shook his head.

The dragon looked at him and he felt it stronger this time. A feeling of sorrow as others had joy. A feeling of pleading.

"That's you?" He stared at the dragon, hoping it was. It was better than thinking he'd lost his mind.

The dragon dipped his head.

Fen was relieved. He wasn't losing his mind after all. "Why now?" He saw an image of the blood oath. Then of two paths. "Great. A dragon that sends riddles." A rush of annoyance hit him. "Fine. I understand you. I've got to make my own choice. But why? You could've let Eddie use the blood oath and you'd always be safe."

A sense of impatience and then the two roads again. Fen sighed.

"Let's go find her. And how about you walk this time. You're too heavy to carry for long."

The dragon walked to the edge of the raised area and waited for Fen to lift him down. Together they walked to the metal door and Fen opened it. Edana leaned against the door to the pen the dragon had come from. Her head jerked up at the sound. She glanced away and wiped her face on her sleeve.

"What do you want?" Edana demanded.

"Spirit cleaning potion."

"Really?" Her expression was cautious.

Fen couldn't resist answering in a sarcasm laden tone. "No."

Edana squealed and launched herself at him. "You're wonderful. You won't regret this. It's the best plan. You'll see."

"I already regret this." Fen untangled Edana from him and held her at arm's length.

"We have to be quick. We can't stay around here much longer or the guards will be back. How did you get into our place?"

Fen described the section of wall he'd come over.

Edana nodded. "I'll meet you there. It won't take me long to get the potion and some money for you."

"Small stuff. Coins," Fen said. When Edana nodded, he said, "And a knife. One that isn't spelled." He pointed to her boots. "And I don't suppose you've got a pair like them that'd fit me?"

Edana grinned. "I don't have long, but I'll see what I can do."

Fen sighed as he watched Edana leave. "I must be mad." He turned to the dragon. "Come on then. Let's get out of here."

Fen grabbed the second blanket as he went through the egg room and nearly made it to the door before he swore. He grabbed a heated rock and a lamp, wrapping each in a blanket, creating a sling from another blanket to carry them. "Come on. We'd better get out of here before the guards come back."

The dragon followed Fen to the wall where he noticed it was shivering. "Why didn't you say something?" Fen took the blanket he wore as a cloak and wrapped it around the dragon. He then pulled the dragon onto his lap and settled the heat stone against him. "Don't go getting sick because I wouldn't have the first idea how to look after a sick dragon."

Fen was glad he didn't have long to wait. It was cold and the dragon was heavy. He didn't know how he was going to get him to the spirit house. As soon as he saw Edana, Fen put the dragon on the ground with the heat stone, both still wrapped in blankets, and went to meet her.

She pushed a heavy backpack at him. "I've drawn a map for you. I've used pictures of common things since you can't read. You'll know the place when you come to it. There's a red rag tied at the start of the lane heading to their gate, one on their gate and one nailed to their front door. Now you need to put four drops of the potion in every room and then two on the doorstep. It doesn't matter which rooms you do first or in what order, as long as the two drops on the doorstep are done last."

Fen nodded. "I'd better go before the guards start searching for the dragon."

"I'll come and see you as soon as I can. It might not be straight away. There'll be many eyes around the place after they notice the dragon's been stolen."

Fen started to turn away.

"Thank you, Fen."

"I can't promise anything. I don't know a single thing about looking after dragons."

"Thank you for giving him a chance. Even when you didn't have to. What changed your mind?"

"Butterfly wings and a choice." Fen swung the backpack on and walked to the dragon. He heard

Edana laugh behind him and smiled grimly. He didn't think there'd be much laughter over the next few days. He still had to face Rhone.

Chapter Four

Fen stared at the red cloth nailed to the front door. The timber house had never been painted and the wood was stained from the damp air that came in off the swamp. A sagging porch sheltered the front door, weeds growing between the boards he stood on.

He stared down at the dragon he'd laid by the front door. Maybe it'd be safer to move him to the fence. He didn't know what to expect when he used the potion.

Fen sighed. Then he sighed once more as he thought of all the sighing he'd been doing that night. Probably as many tonight as he'd done in his fifteen or so years. It was hard to know exactly how old he was because when his mother had died there'd been no one to take care of him and he'd ended up on the streets with other orphans. He vaguely recalled a hand gently stroking his cheek as he went to sleep, calloused and rough from hard work. So he'd probably been less than a handful of years, but he wasn't certain.

"Come on then, let's get you to a safe distance." Fen picked up the dragon and ignored the burning ache in his arms as he carried it to the fence. "Stay here."

The dragon looked at him sleepily then laid his head on his paws and closed his eyes.

"I wish I could do the same." He placed the heat stone against the dragon and turned to the backpack. With an edge of the blanket pulled away from the wizard lamp, Fen was able to see what was in it. Or at least what was on top. A small potion bottle was nestled in some clothes. Beneath them could be anything.

With the potion bottle in hand he headed to the house and stepped inside. A thin layer of dust had settled on the wooden chairs arranged around a fireplace. On the other side of the room was a desk with a handful of parchments and an open ledger covered in numbers. Shelves with some dusty books, a jar of dead flowers, several hand-carved animals and a few shells were beside the desk. Fen opened the bottle and let four drops of the potion fall to the dusty floorboards before he went through the only other door in the room. He froze in the doorway.

It was a kitchen with a large cooking fireplace and an oven set into the side of it. A scarred wooden table and six sturdy chairs were in the middle of the room. Shelves against one wall held wooden plates, pottery cups and tin cutlery. On the top shelf was a single china teacup. Pots and pans hung on hooks near the fireplace. Stairs led above and a door opened to outside. It was similar to most other kitchens of a family several steps up from poor, but not well enough off to be part of the merchant class. He'd seen plenty of them in his many forays for Rhone. But this one had a major difference.

Fen was no novice to the sight of blood, freshly shed or darkened with age. He'd shed enough of it himself, particularly at the hands of Rhone whenever he'd displeased him. But he'd never seen a room so covered in it. The walls were splashed with rust-coloured spray, the floor stained by large puddles. Even the shelves, the contents on them and the table and chairs hadn't been missed.

"No wonder the aunt went crazy." Fen hurried into the room to use the potion. He tried not to think about the dried blood beneath his bare feet or about what mad act would've caused so much blood to be shed.

As soon as he finished, he almost ran upstairs and hoped it wouldn't look the same as the kitchen. He found himself in a small, dim hall. Not knowing if it was counted as a room, he used the potion there anyway. He didn't want to risk the return of a spirit as mad as the one who'd decorated the kitchen. Three doors lead off the hall. One straight ahead and one on either side. He opened the door on his left and stepped into a small room that was obviously a bedroom. He was relieved to see no blood. He used the potion and soon moved onto the next two rooms, both bedrooms about the same size as the first one. Then he hurried to the doorstep. Tilting the potion bottle, he watched as two drops hit the porch floorboards.

Fen stepped back. He didn't know what to expect. All he heard was what sounded like a soft sigh on the breeze. He'd expected more. A loud boom or something. He felt a butterfly wing brush his mind and a feeling of hunger. For a moment he thought it was the spirits before he realised it was the dragon.

"I'm coming," Fen groaned and moved towards the dragon. He placed the potion into the backpack, hoisted it onto his back and then lifted the dragon and heat stone. His arms trembled and the distance seemed impossibly far.

As soon as he settled the dragon by the fireplace in the front room, Fen rummaged through the backpack. "What do dragons eat? Eddie's packed fruit, bread, cheese, some sort of roast meat and something in a covered bowl." Fen undid the string and slid the piece of linen off the bowl. He sniffed at the creamy coloured thickened liquid. "I still don't know what it is." A feeling of pleasure washed over him and with a shrug he gave it to the dragon who started to lap it up.

Fen reached out for a slice of the roasted meat but stopped. He knew what he had to do. And more than likely he'd be retching on the doorstep of Rhone's place after it. He didn't want to waste good food. The dragon looked up at him, a question in his eyes. Fen sighed. Yet again.

"I've business to tend to. I'm not leaving you, but it might take me a while to get back. I'll lay a fire for you before I go. You hide if anyone but Ed comes, you hear?"

The dragon looked at Fen steadily.

"It'd be easier if you could speak. And you need a name too. Do you have one?"

A large body of water appeared in Fen's mind.

"Sea?"

The large body of water narrowed.

"Stream?"

A rush of frustration hit Fen and he almost stumbled backwards. The body of water widened.

"River?"

Approval.

"Like I said. It'd be easier if you could talk. Where did your name come from?"

Fen saw a mother dragon lean over an egg, breathing hot air onto it. She appeared to speak to it and then moved to the next egg. This was the clearest image yet. He could hardly believe he was communicating with a dragon.

"Your ma?"

Approval again.

Fen grinned. "Looks like I might be getting the hang of this. Anything else you like to eat besides slop?"

A tumble of food ran through Fen's mind. Meats of all kinds, fish, eggs, bread, milk, and many other dishes he didn't recognise.

"Fair enough. Now remember, River, stay here. Don't show yourself to anyone. I'll be back as soon as I can." Fen hurried outside and collected kindling and firewood. He laid a fire and lit it with the flint and steel on the mantle then pulled out the blood oath and handkerchief and fed them to the flames. The moment they were consumed he felt no better. There was still the problem of Rhone. Just as bad as a blood oath. He gave River a pat on the head before he went outside.

There was a thin streak of light in the sky. "Rhone's going to be madder than a swamp dragon." He stared at the sky a moment longer before he strode towards the gate, ignoring the ache in his legs that matched the one in his arms.

Chapter Five

Fen paused outside the building that had been his home for most of his life. Like the two storey buildings pressed up against each side of it, what little paint was left on it hung in flakes and all the windows on the ground floor were boarded up to keep other thieves out. The upper level had some gaping holes where shutters had once hung, several boarded up windows and one window where a lone shutter swung in the breeze. Fen barely gave those details a glance. Instead, his eyes focused on the door. An inexpertly painted bright red door, a warning to all that they entered at their own risk.

Fen forced himself up the three rickety steps towards the door. He was surprised to see his hand trembled as he reached out to open it. The door was ripped from his grasp before it was barely open and hands gripped his shoulders to pull him roughly inside and shake him. He stared up into Rhone's fierce green eyes. The man had reddish brown hair, a crooked nose and a few teeth missing. In his other hand he carried the dreaded walking cane, which was pressed against Fen's arm. He didn't need it for walking. It was used as a tool to keep his orphans in line.

"Where've you been? Should've been back hours ago. Can't you see it's bloody daylight? And where's my parcel?" Each question ended with a shake.

"There was someone in there," Fen whined.

"Someone? The guards never stay more than they have to. Not on a night like that. Tell me what happened. You fell asleep, didn't you?"

"No! Soon as the guards went someone shorter went in. I stayed as long as I could. They didn't leave. Not till the guards returned. Then I thought I could go in, but they came back. I don't know what they were doing, but they mustn't have wanted the guards to see them either," Fen said in a rush.

"You lying to me boy?" Rhone growled and shook Fen until he thought his teeth would rattle out of his head.

"N… no," Fen managed to stutter.

Rhone dropped him suddenly and Fen landed in a heap on the floor. He lay still, his cheek resting against the scarred floorboards. He waited for what was to come. Waited as Rhone stood above him, eyes narrowed, anger radiating from him. He tensed then forced himself to relax as he saw Rhone move.

"Get out of my sight." Rhone punctuated each word with a kick or swing of his walking stick.

Fen tried to scrabble across the floor. "It wasn't my fault. I couldn't help it."

"You useless damn cur," Rhone roared.

Fen desperately tried not to cry out as the walking stick hit his cheekbone. It felt like a thousand stars exploded in front of him. The world went slightly grey around the edges.

"One simple job. Walk in. Walk out. Nothing to it." The walking stick thudded at each word.

Fen tried to stumble to his feet but the stick struck his knee and knocked it out from under him. "I tried–"

"No excuses. None! You're a failure." This time Rhone used his boot.

"Please Rhone. I'll do better next time. Give me another chance." Fen's breath came in gasps. He ducked his head in time. His arm took the force of the stick. He thought he heard something crack but his body was in so much pain it was hard to tell. Next it was the boot. "Please." He glanced up, the room spinning with a sickening motion, Rhone standing out starkly as the hole marked walls and the staircase leading to the upper levels shimmered behind him.

"Please. A chance? Never! Do you know how long it took me to set it up? Do you have any idea the money I spent?" Rhone's roar echoed through the place, each word punctuated by another strike. "I could've retired on the money that dragon would've made me."

Fen looked up through one eye, the other rapidly swelling shut. He tasted blood on his lips and tried to suck it off. Even with his mind half numb with pain his first thought was not to leave blood behind. You didn't forget lessons learned with the help of the walking stick. "Don't throw me out." Fen's voice was little more than a whisper.

"That frightens you, does it?"

"I got nowhere to go."

"Good!" Rhone swung the front door open and with a forceful shove of his boot, Fen was pushed out the door to tumble down the steps.

The door slammed shut. The sound echoed in Fen's ears, blending with the ringing already in them. His face rested against the broken and uneven cobblestones and he tried to move. A wave of pain rushed over him as he stumbled to his feet. Dizziness made his vision blur and he staggered. He clung to the splintered wood of the fence, the pain making him gag. There was nothing in his stomach to throw up and soon the retching sounds stopped. Using the fence for support, Fen stumbled down the road.

He knew he had to find somewhere to hole up. The last thing he needed was to be picked up by the town guard, but he couldn't stay in this area. The street gangs watched Rhone's place. The rags he wore and his woollen cap mightn't seem like much, but they were more than some gang members owned. Besides, he knew people who'd been killed for less. Killed because they were easy pickings and it was better to get rid of competition before they became a problem.

Fen spied a familiar alley. He knew it was pointless to look around and see if anyone saw him enter. His vision was too blurred. He had to hope he was in luck. He was glad he'd been with Rhone long enough to know what to say to make him cut him loose. And to cut him loose before he'd beaten him to death. It had still been a gamble. Rhone had his unpredictable moments.

Fen stumbled into some garbage cans and fell to the ground. The sudden sharp pain in his chest made him hold his breath. Broken ribs too, Fen thought as he crawled behind the cans. He huddled against the wall and wished he had the heat stone with him. The stone wall behind him felt like ice.

That was his last thought until a cat jumped onto the can in front of him hours later, jarring him to consciousness. The sudden movement caused him to clench his teeth with pain. He gasped when his jaw ached from the action. He tried to push himself off the ground but found his left arm had been broken and wouldn't work properly. Using his right, he staggered to his feet. The cat snarled at him when he stumbled into the garbage can and Fen hissed back. Even that seemed to take too much effort.

Fen tried to listen to what was happening around him as he swayed down the alley, but one of his ears still rang. Blind and deaf, he thought. May the gods of Kalla watch over me.

Several twists and turns through alleys and backstreets and Fen found a better place to hole up. Or at least he hoped so. It was hard to see and hear if anyone was around.

This time it was a group of young men as they joked and laughed their way to a tavern that woke Fen. He tried to see where they were but couldn't see a thing.

Night, Fen thought with relief. Or I've gone completely blind.

Fen didn't recall his walk back to River. It was a blur of pain. When he staggered in the front door, he checked River was still by the fireplace where he'd left him. The fire had died out, but Fen couldn't do anything about it. Much of the food he'd taken from the backpack had been eaten, but the thought of food made him want to gag. He gently lowered himself to the floor beside River.

Waves of concern rushed through his mind as the dragon looked at him.

"I'll live. Had worse." Fen curled up, sinking into an exhausted sleep.

River snuggled in close to Fen and his heat warmed Fen's cold limbs. As the warmth seeped through him, he relaxed more and his sleep deepened.

Chapter Six

Edana dismounted and tied her horse out the front of the cottage. She knocked at the front door and frowned when no one answered. Cautiously opening the front door, she peered inside. Her heart sank and fear rushed through her at the sight of Fen curled up by the fireplace, the dragon at his back.

"What happened?" Edana ran to his side and crouched by him, hesitantly reaching out to him.

Fen looked blearily up at her. "Not much," he croaked.

"Who did this? My father didn't find you? No. That can't be possible, the dragon would be gone." Edana stared at the dragon. What had happened?

"Rhone. River."

"What?"

"Rhone did this. Dragon called River." Fen closed his eyes again. "Need sleep."

"Rhone came here? He found you?" Edana glanced around, trying to hold back the fear that threatened to swamp her. "We have to leave." She gently touched his shoulder. "Fen." The fear turned to panic when he didn't answer. "Fen? Don't die on me." She held a hand near his nose to feel for his breath.

Fen opened one eye up a fraction. The one that wasn't swollen closed.

"Oh, thank the gods." She felt light headed with relief. "Why won't you talk? Tell me what happened. Was Rhone here?"

Edana felt butterfly wings as the dragon brushed against her mind. Then she saw water. Edana turned to River, trying to figure out what he wanted. Suddenly the picture turned to water in a cup.

"Oh, yes, of course. A drink of water. But what about Rhone?" She felt a wave of reassurance from the dragon. "I hope that means I don't have to worry about him." She rose to her feet and headed for the kitchen door.

"Edana, no," Fen croaked.

"What?" Edana called back.

"Stop her, River."

River uncurled himself and hurried across the room to sit in front of the kitchen door.

"Come on, River. No games." Edana's hands went

to her hips as River tried to herd her away from the door. "You're the one who told me to get him a drink." She looked over to Fen. "Why can't I go in the kitchen?" He didn't answer her. "Fen?" When River nudged her again her arms dropped to her sides. Was that it? Was River trying to get her to check Fen? She stared at him. He lay completely still. She ran across the room and knelt beside him. "Fen? You didn't die this time, did you?" She held her breath. "Fen?"

He groaned and opened an eye. "Don't go in the kitchen."

"Fen." She couldn't keep the worry from her voice. "I'll live."

"Do you want water? There should be a well out the back. I have to get a cup or jug from the kitchen. I can't carry it in nothing."

"Not the kitchen. Promise." His words were laboured.

Edana sighed. "Calm down. I won't go in there. But what am I supposed to use?"

The silence stretched out. Eyes still closed, Fen whispered, "Desk. Shelf. Shell."

"And that makes a great deal of sense," Edana muttered as she rose to her feet and looked towards the desk, her gaze travelling to the shelf. Seeing the shell, she muttered about impossible tasks. She picked it up to find it was about the size of her cupped hand. "This'll take me all day." She stalked out the front door and around the side of the house.

She found the well out the back and lowered the bucket that was tied to the open well with a rope. Once she hauled up the full bucket, she tried to untie the rope. It was frayed and matted at both ends. Impossible. If she cut the rope, it might be too short to draw up water when it was tied back on.

"There goes that idea." She rinsed off the shell and dipped it into the bucket.

Fen lay as still as he'd been earlier and Edana held her breath as she moved closer. "Do you want some water?"

Fen opened his mouth and Edana dripped water from the shell. She stopped when his mouth started to close.

"This isn't going to work. I don't know how you managed to get back here. I don't know how you're still alive. What can I do, Fen? I can't leave you here like this. And how did Rhone get you?"

"Had to go back. Couldn't have... looking for me... find River. Water?"

Edana dripped more water into his mouth as he

opened it. "That's it! I have to do something about this. Wait here. I won't be too long."

"Do I look like… going anywhere?"

Edana smiled. She didn't know if she should laugh or cry. This was more than she'd ever had to cope with. "I guess not." She turned to River who'd curled up beside Fen again. "Do you need anything before I go?" River continued to look at her. "I guess that's a no." She rose to her feet and shook her head. "I can't believe you did this." She stared at him a moment longer. "You're crazy." She would never have been able to bring herself to do the same. Her eyes were drawn to the bruises and swelling. He needed a healer. "I'll be back as soon as possible."

When Fen remained silent, Edana hurried outside, mounted her horse and turned towards home. She kicked her horse into a gallop. Her mind filled with plans.

Her first stop was her room where she gathered items and shoved them in a colourful cloth bag. Next was the kitchen where the cook prepared saddlebags with a picnic lunch for her and a friend. She returned to the stables where her horse waited for her and mounting, she rode for a secluded stand of trees outside the town. She pulled on a dark cloak with a hood and attached a veil, like those worn by the recently widowed, pulled a pouch of coins from her bag and tied it to her belt. Another pouch of coins was tucked into her boots. It was a bad idea to leave all your money in one place. The belt pouch she'd used to put Fen's blood oath in belonged to her father. She'd never dare borrow it during the day when he might have need of it.

"That crazy, crazy boy," Edana muttered, as she made sure her horse was securely tied. The mare was too well known to ride her into town. There was no point in disguising herself to be revealed by her horse, a chestnut with a blaze and four perfectly matched white socks.

Edana stroked the horse's nose. "I won't be too long, girl."

She walked into town towards the home of a healer wizard she'd heard of. One who didn't look closely into the reason she was needed. Edana stood at the front door and butterflies the size of hawks swooped inside her stomach. She thought again of how Fen had looked, one eye so swollen he could barely open it, bruises everywhere, a split and bruised lip covered with dried blood and who knew how many other injuries she'd not been able to see. She'd never seen anyone look like him. He'd seemed barely alive. And he'd sought that beating. Sought it so Rhone didn't come after River. She almost felt ashamed she'd asked him to take the dragon. Almost. River would live. She hoped.

She steeled her courage and reminded herself Fen had probably faced his beating with less fuss. Edana knocked firmly on the door. She waited as minutes passed and knocked again. About to leave, she heard footsteps on the other side of the door.

"Who calls?"

"I need a healer wizard." Edana spoke to the still closed door.

"When?"

"Urgently."

"For you?"

"No. My friend is too injured to travel. I can pay well."

The door swung open to show a white haired woman. Her skinny body was dressed in severe black and her lips were pursed as if she was annoyed by the interruption. "I hope I don't have to travel far. And I need to see your coins first."

"I have a horse outside town, but I'll need to blindfold you once we leave town. I want you to be able to say you didn't know where you went or who you treated."

"It'll cost you more. Come in." The woman

stepped back so Edana could enter. "Do you have a name for me to call you by or are you another Jane?"

"Yileen." Edana used her name that was the most common in the area.

The woman smiled. "A little more original. I'm Daria." The door closed. "Let me see your gold."

"How much?"

Daria grinned. "Not going to beat around the bush are you? No whining about how little you can afford and the cost of things these days?"

Edana shook her head. "My friend needs help immediately. He was beaten. He looks half dead. Can you treat him blindfolded?"

Daria looked at her silently a minute then nodded sharply. She quickly named her fee and said how much up front. Edana counted the money out without argument and dropped it into Daria's hands.

"Wait here. I'll gather what I need." Daria opened a door behind her and slipped through.

It had been too small a gap for Edana to see anything. The room she was in was little more than a small empty box. There was nothing to do while she waited except worry and wonder if Fen would still be alive when she returned. It seemed like an hour, but was less than a quarter of that when Daria returned.

They walked in silence until they were close to

where Edana had left her horse. "I need to blindfold you."

"Get it over with. Mind you watch where you're taking me. If I fall and break my neck I can't help your friend."

Edana nodded and pulled out a blindfold she'd looped onto her belt. She quickly tied it over Daria's eyes and led her along the road. She soon found how difficult it was.

"Can you wait on the side of the road and I'll bring the horse back to you? It's not far," Edana said.

"Hurry up then."

"I'm sorry I had to blindfold you."

Daria snorted. "Not like it's my first time. It's surprising how many have secrets they need kept."

Edana raced down the road. She wanted to be as quick as possible, worried Daria might change her mind. And she was still concerned Fen would die before she returned.

Within minutes, Daria was on the horse and Edana ran in front, the reins clutched tightly in her hand. She was unable to run for long and dropped back to a fast walk. Normally she rode a horse or was taken by carriage if she needed to go anywhere.

Chapter Seven

When they reached the house, Edana helped Daria dismount. "Wait here a moment. I have to check on my friend."

Daria nodded and Edana hurried inside. She went immediately to Fen's side. "Are you still alive?"

Fen opened his eyes for a second then closed them.

"I have a healer here. Don't mention names. We don't want anyone knowing of this and River needs to move away from you. She's blindfolded but I don't want her to accidentally touch him and know he's here."

River flicked his tail like an irate cat. Annoyance poured over Edana.

"I'll watch she takes care of him. She'll help heal him," Edana explained. River rose and moved to a corner of the room. Edana turned back to Fen. "I'll be straight back with her." Fen's eyelids flickered briefly in answer and Edana hurried outside.

Daria's head turned towards Edana's footsteps. "Is that you, girl?"

"Yes. We're ready for you." Edana took hold of the healer wizard's hand and guided her inside to Fen.

Daria knelt awkwardly at his side. She rested her hands on his face. "Someone doesn't like you, boy." Her hands travelled over his body, ignoring his groans and sudden indrawn breaths.

"Careful." Edana's hands clasped and unclasped as she watched.

"Not good." Daria shook her head and clicked her tongue. "Someone wanted to kill you. It's going to cost twice what I said. You didn't tell me someone tried to kill him, only he'd been beaten and looked half dead. He's much worse."

"He was beaten," Edana exclaimed.

"Heal enough for first fee," Fen croaked.

"No. I'll meet your fee," Edana said.

"I'm fine." Fen squinted up at Edana.

"You will be," Edana said firmly. "Now heal him as fully as possible. I'll pay the doubled fee."

Daria nodded and moved her hands back to Fen's face. A soft white glow formed around her hands. Edana watched in fascination as Daria moved her hands across Fen's body. Bruises began to fade, his arm straightened. He gasped as she held her hands over his ribs. Swelling subsided and the only sign he had split his lip was dried blood.

Daria sat back from Fen. "I can do no more. His bones are barely knit together. He needs to be careful. I couldn't take away all the bruises, they were too old. I could've done more if you'd brought me to him sooner."

"Feel like I could run all day." Fen struggled to sit up.

Daria held a hand up. "Stay. You rest a full day. If you come to me in another day, I can knit those bones better. Too much healing and your body can go into shock."

"I'm fine," Fen argued.

"Be it on your head if you kill yourself." Daria rose awkwardly to her feet. "Why not go back and have whoever tried to beat you to death finish the job? You boys are all the same. Too much of a hurry to meet your maker."

"He'll rest." Edana glared at Fen. "If he moves from there before I get back from returning you home I'll beat him to death myself."

Fen grinned up at her. "After all this effort? Not likely."

"Don't try me," Edana warned. "Are you ready, Daria?" She took the woman's hand when she nodded.

Once they reached the horse, she remembered the saddlebags of food. "Can you wait here while I take something in to my friend?"

"If you take too long I'll remove the blindfold," Daria warned. She placed her hand against the horse. "What are you taking?"

"Food." Edana took the saddlebags off the horse and let Daria touch them. "But here, I'll give you your money so you don't have to worry I'm leaving you here without paying." Edana took the bag from her boots, removed a handful of coins, and then handed the bag over.

Daria shook the bag near her ear before she opened it. She sniffed at the coins and touched them. "They seem real enough."

"They are. I'll be as quick as possible."

Edana ran inside and stopped when she saw Fen stood by the kitchen door, his hand on the knob. "What do you think you're doing?" One hand went to her hip, the other held the saddlebag.

Fen grinned. "Gotta use the outhouse."

Edana's eyes narrowed. "Truthfully? And why can't I go in there if you can?"

Fen's grin faded instantly. "It's where they were killed."

"There's no… ah… bodies?" Edana flinched at the thought.

"No. You don't want to see the kitchen. It's a mess. The worse I've ever seen. Blood everywhere. I'd go out the front and walk around if I had the energy."

Edana swallowed hard, all interest in checking the kitchen evaporating. She held up the saddlebags. "I brought you some food. There's even a couple of plates and two cups and a water-skin of orange juice. My nurse I had when I was little always made it for me when I was sick. She said it helps with healing."

"Thanks. Leave it by the fire."

Edana nodded again. She placed the saddlebags where Fen had pointed and smiled when she saw River back in the spot she'd chased him from earlier. "I'd better go. Daria's waiting for me."

Fen nodded. Edana watched him a moment longer before she turned and hurried outside. She felt guilty for what Fen had gone through and couldn't understand why he hadn't yelled at her for the dangerous situation she'd put him in. Maybe he'll tell me off when I get back, Edana thought as she reached Daria's side.

* * *

The front room was empty when Edana returned. She looked around, trying to hold back the fear that started to rise. "Fen?"

"Wait there," Fen called from the kitchen.

"What are you doing in there?" Edana asked as Fen and River came into the front room.

Fen shook his head. "Thanks for the food. It was good. I shared it with River. He eats a lot."

"I forgot how much dragons eat, even when they're little. I just wanted to get him away from there. I don't know if I can smuggle that much out here. I can give you more money."

"More?" Fen looked confused.

"There was some in the bottom of the backpack I gave you the other night."

"I haven't had time to look through it. I was too busy with Rhone."

Edana froze. She waited for Fen to yell about everything that had happened because she'd asked him to steal River. Instead, he moved to the backpack and rummaged through it for the coins.

"Thanks. It should help for a while. I'll have to

think of something else. The river's not far from the outhouse. I guess I could learn to fish."

"That's it?"

"What?"

"I had you steal a dragon from the man who wanted you to steal a dragon and you went back there even though you knew what he was going to do. You knew when you agreed to keep River you were going to have to go back to him, didn't you?"

Fen shrugged. "What's the big deal?"

"He nearly killed you!"

"Wouldn't be the first time."

Edana wailed in surprise, "Not the first time? How could you stay with him?"

"It's easier to swim with one shark than a pack of them."

"What's that supposed to mean?"

"I had two choices. Work for Rhone and put up with his beatings. I was fed most of the time. I had somewhere kind of safe to sleep. The other street gangs didn't bother me. On the street, by myself, I'd have been anyone's prey. I prefer to know where the attacks will come from. Besides, it wasn't so bad. The last boy who failed him didn't make it through the beating."

"How did you?" Edana went white at the thought

of the boy who'd died. She thought how easily it could have been Fen.

"I knew what to say to make him think the streets were a worse punishment."

"How could you have known it would work?"

Fen stared at her, his brown eyes fathomless pools. "I didn't," he said quietly. "It was a gamble. You gave me the chance to get out of there. You gave me a way to be my own master. It was worth the risk. On the streets, seventeen is ancient. That makes me past middle age by street standards. It wasn't that big a risk when you think how close I'd be to the grave if I'd stayed."

Edana shook her head. Her mouth opened and closed several times before she finally found the words she wanted to say. "I didn't realise it was so bad. Why did you stay so long?"

Fen laughed. "And how was I to leave? I have no skills other than that of thief. I look like I've spent my whole life on the streets, and I nearly have. Who wants a common thief working for them?"

"I'm sorry. I didn't know."

"No one does unless they live it."

Edana was once again speechless. "I didn't realise what I asked of you," she said after a bit.

"I know. But I chose to go ahead even though I knew what'd happen."

"How do you feel?"

Fen grinned. "Amazing. Last time it took me a month before I could do much more than shuffle around. I think she's even straightened my nose." His fingers reached up to run along the ridge.

"You still have bruises. They're yellowed, but they're still there."

Fen shrugged. "I always have bruises. I can't get out of the way of Rhone's walking stick every time."

"That won't be a problem now."

"No." Fen's grin came quickly. "I won't miss it."

"I have to return home soon. Is there anything else you need before I go?"

Fen shook his head.

"I'll be back tomorrow with more food. And I'll bring a slate and chalk so I can teach you to read."

"What for?"

"So you can learn how to care for dragons. My father has a massive library on dragon care and other dragon topics. Don't you want to learn how to take care of River?"

"You could read them to me."

"I won't be able to get away every day. My family will wonder what I'm up to," Edana explained.

"Everything's very disordered at the moment because River was stolen. Things will get back to normal soon and I'll have my tutors coming most days. Then I'll only be able to visit one day a week."

"Fine. I'll learn if I have to," Fen grumbled.

"You'll appreciate it eventually. It'll raise your class level. With a dragon and the ability to read, you'll go further than the merchant class."

"I'd be happy to know I'll have food every day."

"Really? This from the boy who was nearly beaten to death to become his own master?"

Fen shrugged and then grinned. "And a few coins in my pocket."

"A large house outside the town, your own servants…" Edana laughed. "I have a feeling the list will grow."

Fen continued to grin at her. "Probably."

"I'll see you tomorrow. We might want to think about horse riding lessons for you." Edana dashed outside before Fen could argue with her and waved breezily over her shoulder as the door shut.

Chapter Eight

Their weeks fell into a pattern. Since Edana's tutors, like most other workers, only worked the mornings on Halfday, she taught Fen how to ride in the afternoon. On Restday, she spent the day with him and taught him to read and write. Firstday through to Fifthday Fen practiced his horse riding on a nag Edana had bought him, worked on his reading and writing, fished for food for himself and River, set traps in the swamplands, laboured over the books on dragons so he could look after River, and slowly turned the house into his own by buying things to place on the shelves and in the rooms.

Fen liked having his own house, even if he didn't own it. He liked having coins in his pockets, even though Edana gave them to him. He liked being able to wear new clothes and not have lice bite him all the time and he didn't even mind bathing once a week before the fire in the kitchen. But most of all, he liked not having to answer to anyone. He was his own person and could choose his own path.

The weeks turned into months and it was Edana's birthday. She was horrified to learn Fen didn't know the day he was born and decided to share her own day with him. So Edana turned fifteen and Fen shrugged and agreed to turn sixteen the same day. More months passed and it was River celebrating his first birthday. He was now starting to fill out and grow. His wings were strengthening and soon he'd be ready to learn to fly.

Fen had been at the house for a year and a half when Edana galloped to the fence and urged her horse to leap it. It wasn't long after they'd both celebrated another birthday at the house. They'd been excited Fen only had another year till he was eighteen and considered an adult with full adult rights. Something Fen believed so completely that even a truthsayer wouldn't be able to argue the fact.

Fen hurried outside to see why Edana was in a rush.

"Oh Fen, I'm so sorry. I never thought it'd happen."

"Whatever it is, it can wait. Walk your horse and put her out the back. I'll meet you in the front room." Fen walked inside before Edana could argue. He'd learned this was the best way to deal with her when she was determined to either do or tell him something.

River looked up from where he lay in front of the fireplace. The flickering flames reflected in his grey scales. There was now no longer any space for the chairs that had originally been there. River might not be as tall as Fen, but he was certainly a lot wider and took up far more space.

"It's only Edana. She'll be in soon," Fen explained on his way to the kitchen.

River put his head down and went back to sleep. So he had enough exercise, Fen took him out at night when there was less chance of anyone seeing him. This meant he slept all morning.

Fen grabbed a jug of juice and a couple of mugs off the kitchen table and took them to the desk in the front room. The wooden chairs from in front of the fire were now in this corner. It made it more cramped, but at least it gave River enough space.

"Fen!" Edana exclaimed as she burst in the front door. "It's important."

"Enough to ride your horse hard and leave her out in the wind?"

"Sometimes I don't think I should teach you

anything. You always find the most annoying time to remember it." Edana flopped into a chair.

Fen handed Edana a cup. "What's so urgent?"

"The old lady who owned this place died. They found her kin and have notified them of the house. They'll be here in two days to take possession."

Fen nodded. "It's time to move anyway. River can barely get through the front door. All the others are too small for him."

"Where can you go?"

"It's probably time to take rooms in town and rent a stable for River."

"But how can you? How will you explain a dragon and no paperwork? I never thought about it when I asked you to take him."

"He's still grey, Edana. I can pass him off as a wild dragon. I've been reading up on dragon laws. I think I can pass the lie test."

"It's death if you're caught lying in a dragon court."

Fen nodded. "I can't discuss it with you. I want you to come and watch me. If it doesn't work, I'll need you to tell River so he can get away. I don't want him being auctioned off to the highest bidder."

"Oh, Fen." Edana stood up and paced back and forth in front of him. "You can't do this. You're not ready."

"We are. It's time."

"I have to go." Edana started to move away.

Fen rose and took a step forward so he could grab her hand and pull her back. "No matter what plan you come up with, I'm using mine. It's time." He stared down at her. She now only came up to his chin instead of being as tall as him. When her chin rose he chuckled. Being shorter than him made her habit ineffective. "There's no point getting annoyed with me."

"Please, Fen. You're not ready. It's only been eighteen months. There's so much more for you to learn. Your hair might be a more fashionable length and you no longer look like a scrawny thief, but there's more to it than that."

"Edana. Stop. I need to know if I can have a life. You've taught me to read, write, ride and find information when I need it. It's my turn to see if I can use what I've learned to move onto the next stage. You were right. I'm not one to stay on the fringes. One day I'll have those servants you spoke about."

"Fine. But I'm not coming to your execution if you fail."

Fen laughed and let go of her hand. "I won't fail."

"No one can lie to a truthsayer. They can see a lie like most people see words on a page."

"I won't be lying."

Edana gasped. "You can't mean to tell them you stole him."

"I'm not stupid."

"But that's the truth."

"What had your father planned to do with him?"

"Kill him."

"Then I saved his life."

"They'll want to know how."

"It's all taken care of. Trust me."

"Huh. Trust you to lose your head."

"I thought you had to go."

"I might as well. I'm wasting my time here."

"Keep an eye on the dragon court notices. I really want you there."

Edana stared at him a moment longer. "When are you leaving?"

"Tomorrow. I need you to introduce yourself to me after the court hearing. Invite me to dinner or something. We need to meet officially."

Edana nodded. "Of course, but-"

"No. No more arguments. I'm set on this course."

Edana sighed. "I'll see you at the dragon courts."

Chapter Nine

Fen was calm as he waited for his turn. The wooden bench with the high back he sat on was uncomfortable. He looked around. The dragon court was full, since everyone had heard about the wild dragon that had bonded with a human. It was a rare event. Wild dragons tended to avoid people.

At the far end of the court was an oak dais where the judge sat, a truthsayer on one side and the court scribe on the other. At the entrance of the room were rows of packed benches and people standing along the rear wall. A low wall ran across the room, separating spectators from the judge's area.

There were several squabbles about breeding rights to be settled before Fen could state his case. He focused on his breathing to keep himself calm. It was the biggest gamble of his life, but one he was confident he could pull off. He'd seen Edana in the crowd earlier. She'd looked worried, almost sickly. He hoped she managed to control herself during the test.

"We now come to the matter of Fenton Walsh and his wild dragon. If you could make your way to the front?"

Fen rose and walked to the bench in front of the judge. He'd chosen the name Walsh after the author of the first book on dragon care he'd read. He knew all citizens had a last name, unlike the poor and homeless. He felt like his name was Walsh. He wasn't the same boy who'd staggered out of the streets the day Rhone had nearly beaten him to death. And he was fairly certain the truthsayer would hear it in his words.

"State your name," the judge said. He was an older man, long since bald, the only hair a tightly clipped grey beard.

"Fenton Walsh."

"How did you come by a wild dragon? Now answer carefully. You do realise the capture of wild dragons is highly illegal," the judge said.

"Yes, Your Honour. And I didn't capture him from the wild. I saved his life," Fen said.

"How did you save his life?" the judge asked.

"I wrote it all down on my application, Your Honour." Fen continued to meet the judge's eyes.

The judge drummed his fingers on the table he was seated behind. "We need to hear you tell us in your own words."

"Like the words I wrote?" Fen mentally urged him to give him the permission he needed.

"Yes."

"You want me to tell you what I wrote?"

"Don't be difficult. Tell us what you wrote on the application."

They were the words Fen needed to hear. He cleared his mind and thought of the words he'd memorised and written on the application. "I was taking a boat up the river when I heard a dreadful noise. It sounded like an animal in pain. I rowed faster. I can hardly believe I rowed to the sound instead of away from it. And then I rounded a corner of the river and saw a wild dragon fighting with a swamp dragon. The swamp dragon was bigger and looked like he was going to win. I raised my bow and arrow, my boat still moving forward. I fired at the swamp dragon and seeing an armed person, it slithered into the water, leaving the dragon on the bank of the river. I rowed forward and saw the dragon was nearly unconscious. He'd been bitten on the nose by the swamp dragon." Fen paused. The crowd was quiet as they all waited to hear how he had become one of the rare few to have a wild dragon.

"I was certain the dragon had no hope of survival. I mean, a swamp dragon bites a human and we all know they go insane. Well, I took the dragon home with me, cleaned him up and nursed him through a fever. I was amazed. Instead of madness, it caused illness. Once the dragon was well, I told him he could go. Instead, I found I had a shadow. I thought maybe he'd get bored of my company and leave, but he didn't. In the end, I had to accept he had chosen me to look after him." Fen remained relaxed, waiting for the judge.

The judge stared at Fen thoughtfully. "Where have you kept this dragon since that day?"

"The dragon's been with me since the day I saved his life."

The judge looked over at the truthsayer. At a nod, the judge turned back to Fen. "We can process your application. What are the details you want on the paperwork?"

"They're all on the application, Your Honour."

"You're happy with these details? You've named the dragon River? Do you want to stick with that name?"

"You heard my story. What name do you think I should call him?"

There was a ripple of laughter from the crowd.

The judge glared at them and they abruptly quietened. He bent his head and filled in the paperwork for Fen. Once he finished he beckoned Fen forward. "I now pronounce the wild dragon, River, to be the property of Fenton Walsh, his owner of choice through his own free will. This dragon cannot be sold, only set free into the wild. Any offspring can be sold as desired." He handed the parchment to Fen. "Any further business?" The judge had to raise his voice to be heard over the excited murmur of the crowd.

Fen tucked the parchment in his leather belt pouch and made his way out of the court. Many of the onlookers followed. They offered him congratulations and handwritten business cards so he could contact them about breeding opportunities. Everyone wanted access to what they thought was a new bloodline, even if River was likely to breed a high percentage of greys. Fen caught a glimpse of Edana through the crowd and slowly made his way to her.

Edana pushed a handwritten card towards him. "My father has a large dragon stable. I'm sure he'd love to meet your dragon. It's not often you hear a wild dragon is tamed. Actually, why don't you join us for dinner tonight?"

Fen glanced down at the card in his hand. "I'm guessing you're not Adalric Serug Perro Renarlo con Vexartian." There was a smattering of laughter through the crowd.

"No, of course not. That's my father." Edana smiled. "I'm Edana Lenita Behira Yileen Renarlo con Crinitie."

Fen returned her smile, remembering the first moment they'd met.

"Allow me to extend an invitation to dine as well young man," an older man said. "You already have my card. I'm Bastian Hamar Majid Omanato con Tenaxalen. I'd be delighted for you to dine with me tomorrow night."

Fen caught Edana's slight nod. "Thank you. Both of you. I'd be pleased to accept your offers."

There was a flurry of invitations and Fen smiled regretfully. "I'm afraid I don't have my planner with me. I'd hate to accept anyone and find myself unable to attend after all. I do know for certain the next two nights are free. But I'm sure I'll catch up with everyone eventually. If you'll excuse me though, I'd like to check on my dragon. He is after all a grey dragon. It's not like I can send blood trackers after him." There was good-natured laughter.

After a few more cards were shoved at him, Fen was able to escape to the stable where he'd left River. The waves of relief the dragon sent Fen were so strong they nearly caused him to stumble. He hurried inside so he could reassure River they had won.

Chapter Ten

Edana's father glared at her. He had the same dark brown hair as his daughter, but his features were broader and his eyes hazel. He was a large man, muscle going to fat since there was little physical work for him to do in the management of his stables.

"I cannot believe you've invited this man to our table. We don't know him. He's probably some upstart forcing himself into our midst."

"Father, there was little else I could do. Bastian had just given him a business card and was making all sorts of noises about entertainments. I was lucky to beat him to invite Fenton Walsh first. As it is he's to dine with Bastian and his family tomorrow."

"Why didn't you tell me Bastian was there?" Adalric and Bastian had been rivals since childhood.

"You didn't give me a chance. I knew you wouldn't want him to be first to invite Fenton

Walsh." Edana grinned at her father. "Everyone knows you don't like to be beaten by him in anything."

Adalric returned her grin. "And why should I? He seems to think he's so far above our family because their family bred dragons before ours. What does that matter when our stables are twice the size of theirs now? Insufferable man."

"Did I do the correct thing?"

Her father ruffled her hair. "You're a quick thinker. Let's hope when you have sons they're as clever. I'd best inform your mother of tonight's plans."

Edana's grin faded as her father left the room. A son! Always a son. A son wouldn't be anywhere near as bright as me, Edana thought angrily. "Oh," she gasped and then quickly ran after her father.

"Father. Father, wait up."

Adalric turned and frowned. "Really Edana, I tolerate your lack of feminine apparel, which is appalling, but I do expect you to act the lady."

Edana slowed to a walk. "I'm sorry father, but that's what I wanted to talk to you about. I don't have anything to wear tonight. I'm sure Bastian's daughter will be decked in her finest when Fenton dines with them tomorrow night."

"Of course. And I'll have the jeweller send you

some pretty baubles to wear as well." With another pat on Edana's head, Aldaric reached into his belt pouch, pulled out a bag of coins and dropped them in her outstretched hand before striding down the hallway.

As soon as her father was out of sight, Edana broke into a run back to her room. She gathered up a few items and stuffed them into her shoulder bag and then dashed to the stables.

Her first stop in town was a dressmaker that did alterations. The place was deserted and the woman behind the counter smiled as Edana entered.

"Mistress Renarlo con Crinitie. You're very welcome to my shop. How can I serve you today?"

Edana pulled an evening dress from her bag and dropped it on the counter. "I wish it refurbished for this evening so it can't be recognised as the same dress. And the details of this transaction are private, Madame Ursa."

The tall thin woman smoothed her already smooth black hair towards the bun it was kept in. "Of course mistress. The House of Madame Ursa is always discreet. You're one of our best customers."

They haggled over price and Edana dropped the coins on the counter as they settled on a time to collect the dress. She hurried outside and walked towards the Eastern Dragon Stables, which is where she'd heard Fen stayed. She slowed as she came closer, hoping to run into him. Then another thought occurred to her.

She thought hard of River and hoped he'd hear her amongst all the other people on the street. She was about to give up when she felt his butterfly touch on her mind. She pictured Fen and the bag of coins she had for him. Minutes later she saw Fen step onto the street.

"Why Mistress Renarlo con Crinitie, what a pleasant surprise it is to see you again," Fen called out. He came to her side. "Might I carry your bag for you? It looks rather heavy to be lugging around in this heat."

"Why thank you, Mister Walsh." Edana pushed the bag of coins secretly into his hand as she gave him the shoulder bag to carry.

"Please call me Fen, Mistress Renarlo con Crinitie."

"Oh, then you must call me Edana," she replied with a grin.

"Really? So very kind of you." Fen's eyes twinkled as he suppressed his own grin. "Ed," he murmured.

Edana looked away. She bit the inside of her lip to prevent herself from bursting into laughter. She turned back. "You are still looking forward to dining with us this evening?"

"I'm counting the minutes."

"Yes and they're rapidly vanishing. I should continue with my shopping."

"Good idea," Fen muttered. "All this rubbish is giving me a headache. Just like it did when you first taught me it."

"Hush, even the cobblestones have ears. The most silent whisper is the one they most want to hear," Edana whispered back before laughing out loud. "Really Fen, you do have a unique sense of humour."

Fen gave her a short bow. "Until tonight," then more quietly, "I have to meet you without the ears." He returned her bag.

"I look forward to your company," Edana replied, and then lowered her voice, "I ride along the river at sunrise tomorrow."

There was the slightest of nods from Fen before he turned to head down the street in the other direction.

Edana sighed and set off to wander through the markets. She'd kept a few coins from the bag of money her father had given her so she thought she might see if she could find anything interesting.

* * *

Edana tried not to glare at her father. The meal was going well, if you didn't count the number of times she'd been ignored and the comments made by her father about the benefits of having a man run a stable. Particularly when Fen mentioned where his dragon was stabled.

"I know the merchant classes do things different and some of their women act like men, but in the royal classes, we allow our women to be themselves. There's no need for them to work like a man."

Edana clenched her teeth together so she wouldn't tell her father he didn't have a clue about how to let her be herself.

"I'm happy with Mistress Bertrisa and the way she runs the Eastern Dragon Stables." Fen glanced towards Edana.

She immediately dropped her eyes to the food on her plate, hiding the anger she knew filled them. She wanted to warn Fen not to argue with her father. He didn't make a good enemy.

"It's a public stable. You need to have your dragon in a private one. I have a private pen coming available in a few weeks. Let me know if you're interested," Adalric offered.

"I'll consider it." Fen lifted his glass of wine and took a sip.

"We might be able to come to terms on breeding arrangements," Adalric continued.

"Wild dragons breed a high number of grey offspring." Edana worried she'd have to rescue more grey dragons.

Adalric turned to his daughter, anger in his eyes. He opened his mouth as if to speak.

"I've read that too." Fen drew Adalric's attention from his daughter.

Adalric nodded. "I'm sure I have a book on that subject in my library."

"Father, you have a book on every subject relating to dragons in your library."

Adalric placed his cutlery on the table as he glared at Edana. "Enough. Eat your dinner quietly or you may retire." He turned back to Fen. "She's a good girl, a little flighty, so she's not accustomed to joining us when we have company."

"Good!" Edana burst out. "But not so good as to have been born the son you need to run your empire."

There was a moment of silence at the table, which

was broken by Edana's mother, Behira. "Edana please see if the servants are ready to bring in dessert."

Behira sat at the foot of the table, silent throughout the meal until now. The only movement was her hand as she occasionally picked at her food. Her blue eyes stared vacantly, her body erect and her light brown hair was arranged in the latest style. The diamond jewellery she wore with her pale blue dress had more fire than she did.

Edana stared at her mother a moment before she rose, hands pressed against the linen covered table. "Yes, Mother." The words came out between clenched teeth as she tried to hold back a flow of angry words. She strode across the room, nearly tripped over her long skirts and her boots came down hard on the wooden floorboards. She froze, hoping the sound hadn't been as loud as she thought it had been. Hoping they didn't realise she wasn't wearing the expected slippers under her gown.

"It might be time to retire to your room for the evening. Obviously the excitement has been too much for you," Adalric ordered.

They'd heard. Edana crossed the room, hearing her father continue as if she'd already left.

"I fear we've spoilt her terribly. But she's my only child. What can a man do?"

* * *

Fen watched Edana leave the room, wishing he could have said something to let her stay. "It seems like she wants to learn more about dragons."

"No. She was showing off. Young girls like to be part of every conversation," Adalric dismissed lightly. "Ah, here comes the dessert."

The rest of the meal passed in conversation about dragons until it was time for Fen to leave. Adalric walked him to the front door. "You must return tomorrow and tour my stables. They're the best in all of Kalla."

"Thank you. I'd like that. I hope to have my own stables one day."

"Ah, a young man with ambition. That's what I like to see." Adalric clapped Fen on the shoulder. "Well, our stables are definitely the ones to see if that's your desire. Midmorning?"

"I'll see you then."

A servant showed Fen to the front door where another servant held his horse's reins. With a nod and a murmured thanks, he took the reins and walked down the gravelled drive. Ahead of him he could see the imposing gates at the entrance to the property.

"Fen," the hissed word came from a tree outside the property.

"Ed?" Fen moved towards the tree.

"What happened after I left?"

Fen grinned. "Nothing at all to worry your pretty little head over."

Edana punched Fen in the arm.

"Hey." Fen rubbed his arm.

"That was for acting like my father."

Fen laughed. "I thought for sure you were going to throw your dinner at him at one stage."

"So did I."

"And when he heard your boots, I thought he was going to explode on the spot."

Edana giggled. "I usually remember to walk softly so they can't hear my boots. I was so angry I forgot."

"You always wear them?"

"I put my dress on over my usual gear."

Fen laughed. "You're certainly original. Hey, what's with your ma?"

"What do you mean?"

"I don't know. A few times I looked over at her and wondered if she'd turned to stone."

"I obviously left a lot out when I was teaching you about etiquette and the royal class. That's how a proper lady of the royal class must act."

"You've got to be kidding. How do you survive it?"

"I don't."

There was silence between them and then Fen said, "I have to be back here by midmorning for a tour of the stables."

"I have to be back before breakfast so my father can rake me over the coals before he turns me over to my tutors for the day. They drive me crazy. Who wants to learn a thousand different ways to ask someone how they are?"

"At least you'll be old enough to go your own way eventually."

Edana laughed bitterly. "How little you know. My father owns me until I'm twenty. He'll marry me off before then. To some man who thinks like him, but he can control."

"I won't let him do that."

"How can you stop him? He has my birth blood. There's nowhere I can hide. I'll see you at dawn." Edana slipped into the shadows before Fen could reply.

Chapter Eleven

After the tour of the dragon stables, during which Adalric once again brought up moving River there, Fen made his way to the Eastern Dragon Stables. He checked there was enough water and put out more food.

"What do you reckon, River? What do you think of this place?" Fen rested his head against River's neck.

An image of the fireplace River had slept near appeared in Fen's mind. River looked at him mournfully.

"One day." Fen gave River a pat before he stepped out of the pen.

"Dragon Lords don't do the work of stableboys."

Fen spun round to see Bertrisa, the woman who owned the stables, leaning against a wall. She had short, spiky blond hair, sharp blue eyes, a wide mouth that went well with her loud voice, and shoulders nearly as broad as a man's.

"What about Mistresses of dragon stables? Shouldn't they learn to leave the hard work to the stablehands?"

Bertrisa laughed and the sound filled the complex. "I'm eccentric. Everyone knows. They'll call you stingy."

"Or overprotective."

Bertrisa shook her head. "Nope. Just cheap." She nodded, pushed away from the wall, and whistled as she went into one of the nearby pens.

Fen took a deep breath and let it out slowly. He didn't need anything else to worry about. He shook his head and put it from his mind. He had other things planned for the day. Like a trip to the market. He needed a better pair of boots and more clothes with all the social events he'd been invited to. He couldn't wear the same outfit every time. A waste of a day. He'd rather spend his time training River.

The market was in the middle of the town with the cobbled streets radiating out from it. The permanent stalls, brightly painted timber huts, were in the middle with a variety of goods from furniture to exotic fruits. The rest of the market encircled the permanent stalls. In the outer ring, some of the stalls were little more than a blanket on the ground with a handful of goods, the seller seated cross legged with their wares. Amongst it all wandered street entertainers, hoping to earn a few coins. The markets were filled with sounds and smells, all vying for attention.

Fen's first stop was at a baker's stall to buy a sticky bun, which he ate as he wandered through the secondhand stalls. A quick movement out of the corner of his eye caught his attention. Rather than turn fully, Fen moved slightly so he could see.

Mouse, Fen thought to himself. What's he doing here? Fen had expected to run into people from his old life, but hadn't expected it to be Mouse.

The scrawny boy was dressed in ragged clothes, wore a floppy felt hat equally full of holes and had bare feet. He brushed against a woman at a stall who put her moneybag away. A red velvet drawstring style that bulged. Fen didn't see Mouse take the bag, but by his movements, he guessed he had. Then Mouse moved on while the lady left the markets with her basket perched on her hip.

Fen threaded his way through the thin crowd in the market so he could keep Mouse in sight. He watched as Mouse bumped against one person, brushed against another and stumbled into a third.

"Oi, thief! He stole my knife," a short, dark skinned man bellowed. A man behind Mouse turned and grabbed hold of him before he could run off.

Fen rapidly slid through the gathering crowd and arrived in time to hear one lady say, "Make him turn his pockets out. Has someone gone for the guard?"

Another called, "He deserves hanging. Don't tolerate thieves around here or they'll all think they can move in on us."

Fen had to do something. He couldn't let Mouse hang. He remembered what it had been like. Hunger, fear and Rhone's walking stick keeping them in line. He took a deep breath, hoping he wasn't making a big mistake. "His punishment is mine to choose." Fen looked around at the crowd.

"And how do you figure that?" demanded the man who held Mouse.

Fen made the only claim he could think of. "Because I've tracked him through the crowd for the last few minutes trying to get close enough to grab him. He lifted my money bag."

"I never. Never seen you 'fore in me life," Mouse protested.

Fen stared at him. "No, I guess you haven't. It doesn't take looking a man in the eye to rob him blind."

There was a murmur of agreement through the crowd.

"How do we know you're not working with him? You look a bit of a shifty one to me," the dark skinned man demanded.

Fen smiled icily. "Since when does a Dragon Lord need to lower himself to petty theft in the market?"

"Hey, I know him. It's the one with the wild dragon," said a teenaged boy with a bad case of acne. "Tell us how you saved the dragon." He nudged the sullen boy next to him. "You should have heard it. Real exciting."

"That has nothing to do with what's going on here," a lady said sternly. Her glare made the boy step back.

"What is going on here?" demanded a guard. His hand rested lightly on the sword belted at his side.

"This thief stole my moneybag. It's red velvet. I demand the satisfaction of dealing with him myself," Fen said.

"I caught him. He took my knife," the dark skinned man complained as he shook Mouse to show he was in his possession.

"I never. Just 'cause I'm not all sparkly clean, they think they can pick on me," Mouse whined.

Fen recalled that tone. He remembered the

desperate feeling that went with it. "Empty out his pockets and you'll see I'm correct."

"And who are you?" the guard demanded.

"Dragon Lord Fenton Walsh." Fen was amazed at the difference his title made to the way the guard behaved. He was glad he'd followed Edana's advice and used the title he was allowed to use since he officially owned a dragon.

The guard turned to the dark skinned man. "And you?"

The man scowled. "Merchant Cadoc Cobbler."

"Ah, a cobbler, that was on my list of things to do today." Even if he hadn't needed them, he still would have said he did in an effort to help Mouse's cause. "Tell me, a sturdy pair of boots, good for around the dragon stables, good for riding in, what will you charge? I don't have time to change boots every minute of the day. They need to be able to stand up to the rough treatment they'd get around a dragon," Fen said.

"Well now, that sort of leather doesn't come cheap," Cadoc began.

"I realise," Fen said. "Quality always has a price."

"Please sir, can we deal with the matter at hand first?" the guard asked Fen.

"Yes, yes, of course. Empty out the thief's pockets

and you'll see he's mine to deal with. Give back the knife to the good merchant here and take whatever else to the guard house where people can claim it when they realise it's gone," Fen said.

"You'll be over to order boots after this?" Cadoc asked Fen.

"Of course," Fen said.

Cadoc nodded and turned to the guard. "I'm happy with that arrangement."

The guard ignored Mouse's protests and quickly found all the items hidden on him. As well as the knife and red velvet moneybag, there were several plain cotton moneybags, a few loose coins, a child's bracelet and a half eaten bun.

Ignoring the whining and complaining from Mouse, Fen asked the guard, "Do you have a length of rope or leather to bind his hands? I don't want him to run off before he gets the whipping he deserves."

"Certainly sir." The guard pulled a length of leather from his belt pouch and efficiently bound Mouse's hands, leaving a piece long for Fen to hold. "He won't get out of that none too fast. Is everything in hand now?"

Fen took the end of the leather. "Thank you. Everything's fine."

Most of the crowd had disappeared. Only Fen,

Cadoc and the two teenage boys were left. The guard nodded briefly to the merchant, bowed slightly to Fen then continued his rounds of the market.

"What are the directions to your shop? I'd best deal with this one before we talk boots," Fen said.

Cadoc gave directions before he strode off through the market. The two boys stayed.

"Can you tell us now?" the first boy asked. His sullen friend stood beside him with a bored expression.

"I have to deal with this scum." Fen firmly gripped Mouse with one hand.

"I'll hold him for you while you give him a flogging," the boy offered eagerly.

"I have my own people for that." Fen pulled a coin from his new moneybag and flipped it towards the boys. "The baker stall with the blue awning still has quite a large selection of sweet buns." Fen nodded in the direction of the baker he'd visited earlier.

"Thanks. When can you tell us the story?" the boy persisted.

Fen grinned at him. "How about next time you see me about come and say hello. If I've got a few minutes I'll tell you all about it."

"Wow," the boy breathed before he grabbed his mate and dashed off.

"I know who you are," Mouse said when they were alone. "And if you think you're flogging me I'll be squealing to everyone. You're no Dragon Lord."

Chapter Twelve

Fen stared at him for a minute. "I guess it'll have to be a hanging then."

Mouse was quiet for barely a second and then he tried to run. Fen dragged him through the market as he kicked and cursed. Mouse managed a few good kicks to Fen's shins but not hard enough to make him let go. He'd suffered worse. At the edge of the market, Fen grabbed Mouse by the throat and pulled him close.

"That was for your benefit. No proper thief goes to a flogging without a protest. Now quit your carrying on."

"And what's this for? You never pushed me round like this 'afore," Mouse whined.

"What else would make a thief settle down? A please and thank you wouldn't. Now when I let you go, drop your head down and shuffle your feet. No more trying to get away. I can't let you go in front of the whole town. Use your brain, Mouse."

Mouse stared back at him sullenly. Stallholders around them pretended not to watch, but Fen knew they strained to hear the conversation. They'd have needed the ears of a dragon to hear the low growl he'd used.

"Do you understand? Are you going to come quietly now?" Fen made sure his voice was loud enough for the nearest stallholders to hear.

"Yes," Mouse hissed.

With a nod, Fen released Mouse's neck. He didn't let go of the leather. Mouse rubbed his neck with his bound hands. Fen knew the rubbing was for effect. He hadn't held Mouse that hard.

When they were well out of town Mouse began to whine about how far they'd walked. Fen ignored him. Mouse whined Fen could let him go. Still Fen ignored him.

"I'm not moving." Mouse pulled back on the leather.

Fen gave a sharp pull and Mouse stumbled forward. "Not far now."

"How far? And where we going? My feet hurt." The whine crept back into Mouse's voice.

"Oh, shut up Mouse."

Mouse fell silent, except for the occasional moan. They finally came to a thick stand of trees and Fen tied Mouse to one of them.

"I thought you were going to let me go."

"I will. In good time." Fen sat down, leaned up against a tree near Mouse and closed his eyes.

"Hey. Don't go sleeping while I'm tied to this tree."

"Quiet." Fen kept his eyes closed. He thought of River. He tried to call him in his mind. Minutes passed. Mouse moaned. Fen ignored him. He focused on River. A butterfly touch brushed his mind. A sense of concern washed over him.

Fen thought of Edana. He showed River her in her usual clothes and then in the widow's outfit. Next he thought of the blood oath he'd signed and then visualised the blank parchment. He pictured where he was and sent a feeling of urgency to River.

River sent a wave of assurance before the butterfly touch was gone. Now he had to wait and hope Edana would understand. He kept his eyes closed a little longer, wanting to postpone the talk he needed to have with Mouse. Fen finally opened his eyes to stare at Mouse.

"What? Not sleepin' now? What we waiting here for?"

"What were you doing in the market on a light day? Do you have a death wish?"

"Rhone sent me."

"Why?"

"Getting too old."

"He wants to get rid of you."

Mouse nodded. "He said I was allowed the markets Firstday to Fifthday. Halfday and Restday belong to some of his other boys. Till I can show him a good haul, I don't get my old grounds back. I nearly had it today. Then that merchant," Mouse spat the word out, "had to ruin things."

"How badly do you want to leave Rhone? If I can promise you work, food and clothes will you stay with me?" It would have been easier to advertise for a stablehand, but he had to do something with Mouse.

"What sort of work?" Mouse asked suspiciously.

"Stablehand."

"I'm no one's lackey."

"Dragon stable."

"Cor! You weren't spinnin' a story earlier? How'd that happen? Didn't Rhone send you after a dragon? Didn't he flog you for not getting one? How's it you got one after all?"

"Mouse. Focus. Can you work for me as a dragon stableboy? I can offer you a better life than what

Rhone offered, but you'll have to sign a blood oath. No matter which choice you make today, a blood oath will be involved."

"No way. Not chancing my blood boiling." Mouse shook his head.

"You have exactly two choices. You hang or you take a blood oath. I'm not having you ruin my plans. I can't have the wrong people finding out where I came from."

"That's lovely, that is. An old friend an' all. What you want to kill me for? I won't blab."

Fen tried to ignore the need to shake Mouse. "I don't want to kill you. And I won't. I'll hand you over to the town guards to execute. I don't want to, but there are too many things at stake. I want you to take a blood oath. It's quite simple and one day I'll take it off you. There'll be less chance of you dying from breaking it than living in Rhone's dubious care."

"Speak normal. Anyone'd think you were using a foreign language with some of the words you spit out."

"Mouse. Quit stalling. I need you to make a choice. Blood oath or town guards?"

Edana came into the trees. "Oh, I don't know. He doesn't look worth the effort either way. I say we throw him in a sack with some rocks, tie it up tight and dump him in the river. Much less effort." Her widow clothes prevented Mouse from seeing who she was.

"Blood oath," Mouse squealed. "Keep her away from me. Never liked no widow women anyhow."

Fen nodded. He moved over to Edana, hoping she'd brought the parchment with her. She had and quickly gave it to him.

"River gave me a fright when he caught me. I didn't know he could reach that far. My tutor thought I was suddenly ill. So I guess it worked well, but don't let him do that too often."

Fen moved her further away from Mouse to make certain he couldn't hear their softly spoken conversation, noticing Edana's horse tied to a tree further away. "I had to do something. He's from my old life. I can't have stories getting back to Rhone yet. I'm not ready." It took him only moments to tell Edana the basics.

Edana nodded. "Make sure you don't write anything on this parchment you wouldn't feel safe having another read. You remember how I worded it?" At Fen's nod, Edana continued. "Here's some more money. I was worried the problem was more complicated than River showed me." She handed over a moneybag.

"Surely your father must notice the amount you've spent without anything to show for it." Fen dropped the bag into his left boot.

"I've never had much to show for the amount of money he's given me over the years. Us spoilt brats have a tendency to spend money like it's water."

Fen chuckled. "You're only a spoilt brat occasionally these days."

Edana smiled momentarily. "What are you going to do with the moneybag Mouse stole?"

"I can't give it back to the lady. I'd probably be accused of being an accomplice."

"You could donate it to one of the temples for the poor."

Fen nodded. "Sometimes it's strange I no longer have to lift moneybags for Rhone."

"You won't have to ever again." Edana glanced towards her horse. "I have to go home. If I'm caught out while I'm supposedly in bed sick there'll be a lot of questions."

"Thank you. Sorry I had to drag you into this mess. I could think of no other way to deal with it."

"You'll have to tell me all the details later."

Fen smiled. "Early morning ride tomorrow? I can tell you the rest then."

With a quick nod Edana left.

Fen walked back to Mouse. "Blood oath it is. Let's get this over as quickly as possible. I still have to see a merchant about a pair of boots today. You're an expensive problem, Mouse."

"Humph. Brought you a fat purse more like," Mouse grumbled.

Chapter Thirteen

"He wasn't quite what I had in mind when I said you needed a stableboy."

Fen looked up to where Bertrisa stood in the doorway of River's pen. He grinned. "I like him. Got an attitude as smooth as sand, as agreeable as a cornered rat and a sense of fashion that puts us all to shame."

Bertrisa chuckled. "The gods forbid anyone else should dress the same as him."

When Fen had taken Mouse shopping for clothes the day before, the boy had chosen bright red boots, a green shirt, orange trousers and a purple felt hat. He'd swaggered around the stables as soon as he'd washed and donned his new clothes.

"You do realise if anything goes missing around here the finger will be pointed at him," Bertrisa said.

"Impossible. He's sworn a blood oath not to steal

anything from anyone." Fen didn't also say 'unless I give him permission' as he had during the oath. It had been easier to add that rather than keep arguing with Mouse about the wording.

"That's good. Makes things a lot easier. Why a blood oath? A bit unusual wouldn't you say?"

"I have to make unusual decisions. Grey dragons can't be blood tracked."

Bertrisa nodded. "That's something I didn't think about. I'll mention those two bits of information in a few ears. You shouldn't have any trouble with your choice of stableboy."

Fen nodded slightly in answer. Bertrisa stared at Fen a moment longer before she gave him a deeper nod and left. A wave of reassurance swept over Fen and he looked at River. Fen moved forward so he could lean up against the dragon who was now much taller than him.

"It'll be fine," he assured him.

River sent him a picture of a stone fireplace.

Fen smiled. "We'll have to see what Bertrisa has to say."

Wooden floorboards were added in front of the fireplace.

Fen laughed. "I think that might be pushing things.

You know how funny people are about dragons and materials that burn easy."

Mouse came in, a wooden bucket three quarters filled with water. "Don't see why I have to lug all this water."

"If you filled the bucket up the job would be quicker."

"And have my new clothes soaked by the water splashing over?" Mouse sounded horrified.

"Water won't hurt them."

Mouse snorted. "That's what you think."

"I'll leave you to it. I've got things to do this morning."

"Not mornin' yet."

Fen ignored Mouse and made his way to the horse stables where his old nag was kept. He was soon on his way to meet Edana for their early morning ride.

"We need to get you a better horse," Edana said in greeting.

"I like this one."

Edana grinned. "Not the right look for someone as important as a Dragon Lord."

Fen patted his horse's neck. "Don't listen to her."

"Dragon Lords will keep inviting you to their gatherings. You can believe me when I say people will talk if you arrive on an old nag. Servants are the worst. Far more snobbish than their masters."

Fen sighed. "There are too many rules in your world."

"I thought it was your world too."

"Only because I've pushed my way in."

"How's your new stableboy working out?"

Fen laughed. "If you skip the word working, he's doing fine. He doesn't mind the night errands, it's the early mornings he curses."

Edana leaned forward and handed Fen a folded piece of parchment and a bag of coins.

"Now what?" Fen took them.

"Directions of where to get your new horse. I've written down the names of the ones I thought suitable. Showy looking but suitable enough for the most incompetent rider. There's enough money there to pay for your choice as long as you do some haggling. If they charge you more, they're trying to rip you off."

"Incompetent rider?"

"You're not really," Edana said with a grin. "But they are good horses. They shouldn't balk at being around a dragon."

"Any other orders for the day?"

Edana laughed. "Well…"

"I should have known."

"No. This is important. I overheard my father talking to his lawyer last night."

"Overheard?" Fen raised an eyebrow.

"I might have been somewhere suitable to hear what was happening when a servant announced the arrival of my father's lawyer."

"And what has his lawyer got to do with me?"

"My father's trying to take your dragon."

"What? How can he? I have paperwork proving he's mine." Fen's hand went to his waist where a cloth was wrapped around him to hide his paperwork.

"You're not an adult yet. If you weren't considered an orphan, you wouldn't be allowed to own River."

"Then how can they get him since I am an orphan and I do have the paperwork."

"By you becoming his protégée. It's a bit like if he'd adopted you. So, whatever you do, don't let him talk you into stabling River. It could be seen as you accepting a position as his protégée. As long as you pay your own way and use public stables or have your own stables, you'll be fine. It doesn't matter who makes the offer. Anyone can use the same law to take River from you."

"Great. Any other laws I should know about?"

Edana shook her head. "None I know of, but I didn't even know that one."

"So next time he asks I say no. It's not like he can force me to use his stable."

"Not exactly. He might make it impossible for others to let you rent space at their stables. Then you'd have no choice but to use a private stable. You need to tell him you're considering it. Make him wait for an answer."

"I can't do that forever."

"I know. But it'll give us time to think of something we can do."

"Any other wonderful news for me?"

"No." Edana shook her head. "I'm sure that'll be enough to ruin your day."

"You've got that right."

"I have to go. If I'm late for breakfast my parents will wonder what I'm up to of a morning. If I make very few waves, they don't pay any attention to me and I can run my own life a bit."

"That doesn't sound like much of a life to me."

"And yours was much better? Getting beaten near to death for the slightest reason?"

Fen shrugged. "I guess now we've done something about my life it must be time to sort yours out."

"Impossible. I've already told you that. I have to

go. I'll see you in the morning. On your new horse." Edana turned her horse in the direction of home and kicked her into a gallop.

Chapter Fourteen

Fen's day was filled with horse buying, organising room at the stables for it and finding a suitable outfit to wear to that night's dinner party.

After the dinner party Fen began to dread having to sit through more of them. He'd never been so bored in his life, not to mention needing to watch everything he said. And he knew he had invitations to many more parties and events being held over the next few weeks by different Dragon Lords. He also had very little choice other than to attend, as he couldn't afford to upset any of the Dragon Lords. He didn't have the wealth they had. Most of them were of the royal or noble classes. Dragons were nearly always sold privately and the upper classes didn't want the lower classes in their ranks.

Over the weeks Fen had many offers by the Dragon Lords regarding the stabling of River.

Remembering Edana's advice, he put them off. Offers poured in when they found he was considering his options.

A few months passed. The nights were filled with social events, the mornings riding with Edana and the days with River. The dragon continued to grow and his wings strengthened and matured. He turned two and it seemed as if overnight his ability to fly began to improve. Fen read books on how to teach dragons to fly the complicated patterns for racing and when Bertrisa caught him in the pen reading one day she started to offer her own advice.

They were in the flight arena of the Eastern Dragon Stables late one afternoon when Edana's father, Adalric, called. He stood beside Fen who leaned against the rail that was to keep onlookers out of the dirt arena where the dragons landed and took off. Afternoons were saved for new flyers when only one at a time could be in the arena. Unlike most dragons being trained, River didn't need a handler in the arena to tell him what to do. Fen thought of what he'd read in his books, put it in picture form in his mind and projected it to River.

"Who's training the animal?" Adalric leaned against the rail.

Fen turned to Adalric, annoyed at the interruption. "He's practising."

"You can't throw him in the arena and expect him to know what to do."

"I don't. He's had training. Now he's practising." Fen didn't want anyone to know the full depth of his bond with River. Everything he read showed how unusual it was.

"How long has he been training for?"

"A few weeks." Fen watched the clumsy take off and showed River where he'd gone wrong. "Sorry, what did you say?" Fen looked over to Adalric who stared at him as he waited for a reply.

"Not bad for so little training. It looks like he might be a fast one. But they say the wild ones often are."

Fen tried not to sigh. He wished Adalric would go so he could finish his session with River. They had so little time each week in the flight arena. They weren't the only ones who wanted to practice flying the obstacle course.

"I've read somewhere all greys are fast. Both tame and wild," Fen said.

"Where did you read that? What rubbish. How can anyone say that when no one keeps tame greys? Just because they're a throwback to their wild cousins, it doesn't mean they have any other of their traits."

Fen quoted the dragon book he'd read the information in. "Why do you say no one keeps tame greys?"

"Everyone knows you don't want to taint a line with that gene. It's different if they're wild. It's good to have new blood brought into the lines. Eventually as you breed along the line from the wild grey you go from half the hatchlings grey to the odd one or two in every few generations, but you have that anyway."

Fen felt a rush of anger at Adalric's attitude towards dragons. River sent a calm feeling towards him to help him rein in his emotions. "What brings you to this part of town?"

"We're holding a dinner party on Halfday of next week. We'd be delighted if you attended. Let me know sometime in the next couple of days."

Fen nodded. "I'm fairly certain I have nothing on that evening, but I'll check my planner later and let you know."

Adalric looked towards River. "You know, if you were in private stables you'd find there was more time available for you in a flight arena. He could do with longer hours in there each day. Have you thought anymore on my offer?"

Adalric had regularly sounded him out over the past few months and Fen had the impression Adalric's patience was wearing thin. Fen nodded. "But I've had so many offers it's been difficult narrowing it down."

"You said that last week. Surely it can't take you so long to make a decision. This indecisiveness is not a healthy trait."

"I've narrowed it down to a handful of choices. You're one of them. And your neighbour Bastian. Your two offers are the most tempting. You must understand it isn't a decision to be made lightly. I only have one dragon and I have to think of what's best for him."

Bertrisa chose that moment to enter the flight arena and signal his time was finished. "If you'll excuse me, I have to see my dragon returned to his pen."

"That's what stableboys are for," Adalric said.

"He's a wild dragon. I'm sure you've read about some of their unusual ways. How they rarely take to more than one person. I'm afraid he barely tolerates other people, unless I'm there to assure him all's well." Fen was grateful to think of a way to get rid of Adalric. He didn't know if this was true of wild dragons, but he'd read it. He did know it wasn't true of River. He only disliked people Fen disliked.

"I hope to see you at my dinner party. I expect you should have figured out your choice by then."

Fen knew this was his deadline. "Certainly. You'll be one of the first to be informed."

Aldaric stared at Fen a moment longer before he turned abruptly and left the arena. Fen looked towards River and mentally called him.

"He's not the type of man you should upset."

Fen turned around, surprised to see Bertrisa was back. "I'm trying not to."

Bertrisa smiled wryly. "Some men are easily upset."

"So I'm beginning to think." Fen glanced up at River who had come to stand beside him. "Come on, let's get you back to your pen." They left the flight arena with a nod of greeting to the next dragon trainer who waited to use it.

Chapter Fifteen

Fen sat on his horse and waited for Edana to join him. He looked upwards with a frown as the sky started to fill with the vibrant colours of the rising sun. Some mornings he waited in vain for her to arrive. He had hoped today wouldn't be one of them. He'd informed Adalric at his dinner party the night before that he'd continue to use the public stable. Adalric had been polite but incredulous. He'd pointed out all the drawbacks of public stables without appearing to be pushing his own stable on Fen. But Fen was sure he'd seen a glimmer of anger in the depths of his eyes. He'd hoped Edana would be able to tell him what her father's next move would be.

He was about to give up and head back to town, when he saw a rider gallop towards him. He was relieved to see it was Edana.

She pulled up beside him. "Let's go. I need to keep

my horse moving after how hard I've ridden. I also don't have much time."

"I was beginning to think you weren't coming." Fen urged his horse into a walk and drew alongside of Edana's horse.

"So was I. You certainly know how to cause a commotion. You should have heard my father after you and all the guests left last night." Edana grinned. The grin quickly faded. "It's not going to be pretty."

"What's he planning?"

"Exactly what we expected. He's going to make it impossible for you to stable River anywhere so you'll be forced to come crawling to him. Everything's going to be impossible for you. I'm sorry." Edana reached out to touch Fen's arm. "I don't know what to do."

Fen nodded. He rapidly thought of ideas and just as quickly dropped them. "I'm not letting them get River. He's mine. I went through too much to get him. Besides, they wouldn't treat him right."

"With how quickly he's been learning to fly and how smoothly he's moving in the air, he'd be treated royally by whoever had him."

"I don't care. No one'll have him. And they wouldn't keep him once he couldn't compete or breed. You know Dragon Lords rarely let dragons die of old age. Dragons live too long for them to bother."

Edana sighed. "Fen-"

Fen shook his head. "If the plan doesn't involve River staying with me, forget it."

Edana fell silent.

"I've had worse problems."

"Unless your dragon has stabling, public or private, he can't be entered in any of the dragon competitions. The races, the events, the battles, none of them."

"Is there a definition of what a private stable is?"

"I can get a hold of the Official Dragon Competition Rulebook."

"I'll get my own copy."

Edana shrugged. "Suit yourself. You'll find it at any of the bookshops out near the competition grounds. What are you planning?"

"I don't quite know yet, but there has to be something. I'm not letting them beat me."

There was a strong brush against their minds followed by a fierce feeling of agreement.

"And they're not going to beat River either," Fen said fiercely.

"I didn't know he was following us with his mind. Does he often listen in?"

Fen grinned. "He doesn't trust me not to get into trouble without him there to look after me."

"I'm not surprised." Edana momentarily returned Fen's grin. "I have to go. I can't be late or my tutor will complain to my father. And he isn't in the mood to be generous today."

"Tomorrow morning?"

"I hope so. It was difficult to sneak out this morning." Edana turned her horse around and headed for home.

Fen turned towards town, his mind on the problem of what he could do.

After hunting down the book he needed, Fen returned to River's pen. He ran his hand along the dragon's neck, comforting and drawing comfort from the action.

"No fireplace now?"

Fen heard the words whispered in his mind. He glanced around. He was alone with River. "That was you? Speaking in my head?"

River lowered his head. His eyes blinked in agreement.

"But how?"

River stared at Fen. A few minutes later, a rush of confusion washed over Fen. *"New. Difficult."*

Fen nodded. "I guess you did once tell me you

would." Fen reached out and stroked River again. The dragon closed his eyes and waves of contentment washed over Fen.

"You find plan." A feeling of certainty followed River's thought.

"I hope so."

"Are you still talking to that dragon of yours?" Bertrisa appeared in the doorway of the pen.

Fen smiled slightly. "Only way to have an intelligent conversation around here."

"That's not surprising considering your stableboy."

Fen's smile became a grin. "He isn't that bad."

"I'm not getting into that argument." Bertrisa's smile disappeared. "So, who'd you annoy? Must've been someone pretty important."

Fen's smile faded instantly. "Adalric."

"Adalric as in Renarlo con Vexartian?"

"Afraid so."

Bertrisa whistled. "You don't do things by halves. Well, he's putting the pressure on me, through a third party, to turf you out. I'm afraid I can't help you much. The most I can do is hold out for five days. Will that give you enough time to find somewhere else?"

Fen shook his head. "No, but I appreciate the help. I don't suppose you've got any miracles stored away?"

Bertrisa laughed. "Not the size you need. Why'd you go and mess with him anyway?"

"He decided to mess with me. He's hoping I'll come to him looking for stabling."

"And the problem would be?"

"I'm not eighteen, I'm an orphan and a potential protégée."

"Why that slimy snake! Don't you dare give into him. I'll see what favours I can call in. Don't hold your breath though. You're certainly in an impossible situation."

Fen watched as Bertrisa strode away. He leaned against River. "And don't I know it."

Chapter Sixteen

One more day left, was Fen's first thought when he woke. One day. He couldn't stop thinking about it. He didn't know how he was going to get through the day. The knowledge that River counted on him and Edana was probably getting ready to go riding was the only reason he stumbled out of bed. He shook Mouse, who slept on a mattress in his room.

"Not mornin' yet," Mouse mumbled.

"Get up and get River's food." Fen wasn't in the mood for Mouse's continual complaints.

"Aren't you a happy one today?" Mouse glared at him as he rolled out of his blankets. "What can you expect messin' with royals?"

"Enough."

The ride with Edana didn't go much better. Fen was too angry with Adalric to say much and Edana felt responsible.

"I should never have asked this of you. I should've let you steal any old dragon and you wouldn't even have thought of stealing it off your old master," Edana said.

"Shut up, Edana."

"Shut up yourself."

Fen closed his eyes for a second. "I'm sorry. And it's not your fault."

"He's my father."

"Yeah, but you warned me what to expect. I managed to string him along for ages. I'm just not sure what I can do next."

"I wish I could get a hold of enough money for you to build your own stables."

"Eventually River will be able to earn that sort of money."

"Not if he doesn't have a stable to stay at during his events."

"I guess I'll have to live in the swamps until I'm eighteen and no one can take him off me."

"But how will you live? You'll probably be bitten by a swamp dragon. You have to come up with a better plan."

"Edana. Stop. I can't think about this right now. I've thought about it constantly, trying to figure something out. I need a few minutes without worrying."

"Sorry," Edana said softly. "I'm worried too."

"I know."

"I'll race you to that tree." Edana called out as she kicked her horse.

Fen laughed at her obvious ploy and urged his horse to follow. When they both reached the tree, Edana first, they slowed their horses.

"Did that help?" Edana asked.

Fen smiled slightly. "I'm glad we met. Whatever happens. This is the life I was meant to have, not the one I had before."

"You really mean to take to the swamps?"

Fen shrugged. "If that's my only choice. I'll be waiting for you tomorrow. I'll let you know where to find me then."

Edana frowned. "But Fen-"

"No. We'll talk about it tomorrow. Come on. You'd better head home before you're missed."

Edana sighed. "I guess you're right. But you're not getting out of talking tomorrow."

"I'm sure I won't."

When Fen arrived back at the Eastern Dragon Stables, Mouse leaned against a wall in River's pen as he ate a sweet bun. "Dragon lady wants to see you.

In her office. Will we still get these when we leave?" Mouse indicated the bun.

"Probably," Fen said, still distracted by his problem.

Bertrisa's office was a tiny room cluttered with several overflowing bookcases and a desk buried under mounds of paperwork. It was behind this mound she was seated, trying to do her bookwork.

"Good. I was wondering when you'd get in." She held out a parchment. "Take this and go and talk to the man at this address. It's about the best offer you're likely to get. He's in it for the revenge. I still wouldn't completely trust him. I don't believe in trusting anyone."

Fen stared at the parchment.

Bertrisa shook it. "It's not going to bite. Take it and get out of here. Time's wasting. You can't stick around here remember. I've my own head to think about."

Fen took the parchment. He read it. "Who's Hanun Carson?" The name was followed by an address outside the town in an area where the lower levels of the upper classes lived.

"A man with an axe to grind."

"Why?"

"I'll let him tell the story, but let's say not all his relatives were overjoyed by his birth and he'd do anything to annoy the hell out of them. But that doesn't mean you should trust him. He has one dragon and no hope of another. Yours might be too much of a temptation for him. Keep it in mind when you meet up with him."

"Why would I bother with him then?"

"Because beggars have little to choose from. Play your cards close to your chest. See what's on offer. You might be able to turn it to your own advantage. Going to see him won't cost you a thing."

"I guess not." Fen tucked the directions into his belt pouch.

"I'm sorry you can't stay. Unlike some I've put up with you haven't been any trouble. Even your stableboy's less a problem than some of them."

Fen headed back to River's pen. "I've got to see someone. Keep an eye on River."

"Do I have to move from here to do it?" Mouse, sprawled in a pile of straw, peered at Fen from under his arm that rested across his eyes.

"I guess not." Fen looked at River. *"Watch for trouble."* It was becoming easier to communicate with River now he was learning to speak with his mind.

River sent him a wave of reassurance.

"I'm going to see a man about some options for us," Fen

told River. He stepped forward and reached up to rest his palm against the warmth of River's neck.

"Anyone'd think you were waiting for him to talk," Mouse grumbled.

Fen smiled at River, feeling his amusement. "I'd get more sense out of him than you."

Mouse grunted in reply.

Chapter Seventeen

Standing on the doorstep of a large house, Fen stared at the man who answered his knock. Even though his hair was as white as snow and his face lined with wrinkles, he stood straight and tall, his blue eyes sharp. To Fen, it appeared the lines and white hair were more a sign of a hard life than age. The man seemed to be in his early fifties.

"I'm here to see Hanun Carson."

"And who are you?"

"Fenton Walsh."

"Ah, the dragon boy. Come in then." The man held the door open wider.

"My horse–"

"I'll send someone to deal with it," the man interrupted.

Fen followed the man inside. They ended up in an airy room that looked onto a paved courtyard. As soon as they were seated, the man rang a bell and a servant appeared immediately.

"Yes, sir?"

"Refreshments. And see to the boy's horse."

The servant bowed and left without a word.

"You're Hanun Carson?"

"Most days. And depending on who you ask. Quite a few say I don't deserve to carry the name."

"I've been told you have a proposition for me."

"Ah, the impatience of youth."

"Yes well, we like to get things done rather than grow old waiting for them to happen."

Hanun chuckled. "A boy with a tongue in his head. Considering your circumstances I'd think you'd be grateful to even have an option."

"I have options. I'm not keen on any of them at the moment, but I still have them."

"I wouldn't want to give up my dragon either."

"That's not my only choice."

"So what are your other choices, boy?"

Fen smiled. "Now that would let you know where you stand in our negotiations, wouldn't it?"

Hanun stared at him thoughtfully. His servant came in during the silence and Hanun pointed to the small table beside his seat. After the servant had gone, Hanun started to nod. "You might do after all."

"I need more than your approval before I can agree with that comment."

"So you do. Tea? Cake?" Hanun waved his hand towards the tray the servant had brought in.

"Thank you." Fen waited with a semblance of calm to be served.

"I guess you'll want to hear my story. It has a great deal of bearing on my offer. Or at least the reason for it."

"That'd be helpful." Fen took the teacup Hanun held out.

Hanun nodded thoughtfully. His eyes lost their sharp look. "I was raised for the first ten years of my life by my mother and I had her family name. It wasn't until I started my schooling I realised how unusual that was. We were lower merchants so I wasn't teased too badly. I fought back a few times and wasn't bothered much after that. But it made me question my mother. Made me want to know about my father. It took years. I'd get a bit of information each time I badgered her. I finally pieced it together."

"And the name some people don't think you worthy to bear?"

"Ah, my first name. My mother named me for my father. The man who for years I thought didn't want me. The man who didn't know I existed. My mother went to tell him she was pregnant but instead ran into my grandfather. He was appalled and paid her to leave. She didn't want to accept the money, not until my grandfather explained my father was to be married in eleven days. She was devastated. She took the money because she was so dazed when he placed it in her hands she didn't know it was there. She used it later to send me to school. It was hard having a child all alone."

"What about her parents?"

Hanun shook his head. "Long dead. They had her late in life. By the time she'd met my father, she'd buried them both. She was alone. No brothers or sisters, aunts or uncles. She did everything possible to raise me right. And when my father found out, he wanted to take me from her. I refused. I was glad after I met my half brother. For a while I was thrilled. I had no brothers or sisters. And here I had one six months younger than me. He wasn't thrilled." Hanun fell silent.

"What happened?" Fen prompted.

"He did everything possible to cause trouble for me. That made me more determined to stick around. We're a stubborn lot us Carsons. Always have been, always will be. Didn't matter what he did. I wouldn't let him win. Then he was given his first dragon for his eighteenth birthday. I wasn't. He finally had something I couldn't compete with. That was the first time I argued with my father. Even when I refused to live with him we didn't argue. He bought me this home, he showered me with gifts, but I refused to be satisfied. I wanted my own dragon. My younger brother had one and I was denied one because of my low birth."

"I've been told you have one."

"Patience youngster." Hanun gestured towards the tray. "More cake?"

Fen shook his head.

"Now, where was I? Ah, yes. My father died. I had a lawyer on my doorstep telling me he'd left me some money and a gift. It was a young female dragon called Pearl. I had what I'd coveted for so long. But in the process I lost my father. And while we were arguing. I regret that. But I don't regret the animosity between my brother and I. He was named for our grandfather and is the same sort of man. I'm glad I never met our grandfather. He died while I was young. But anyway, that brother of mine, he was here the next day offering me money for my dragon. He tried everything he could to get her. He even tried to steal her. He failed. You should have seen his anger when I raced her. Never placed better than third on four occasions. It was too expensive to continue when she couldn't place in a paying position. I tried to breed her. Thought I could make money doing that. No one wanted to. They couldn't keep me out of the competitions, nothing in the rules to keep me out. But they could all refuse to associate with me or let my dragon mate with theirs."

"None of them? They all banded together?"

"All of them. I thought about letting her mate with the wild dragons, but any female dragons that escape to the wild never want to return. I didn't want to lose her. She still has years of breeding left in her. Obviously not as many eggs in each clutch at her age, but she can still lay eggs. I don't believe in killing a dragon because they're too old for competing and not as good at breeding anymore. My Pearl will outlive all of us."

"Is that what you're looking for? A dragon to breed with?"

"I've also heard rumours about the speed of your dragon. I want to see an outsider win in the races. I want to see my brother's face when one of his gold-winning dragons come second to a commoner. I'll give you bed and board, I'll sponsor your dragon's fees for the events and I'll share the dragons with you from the hatchings."

"And what'll it cost me?"

"What are you willing to give in return?"

Fen laughed. "I wasn't born yesterday. Give me your offer. I'll let you know what I think about it."

"We split the winnings after expenses. We share in the profits from selling the dragons when they're old enough."

"And if we can't sell them?"

Hanun's chuckle held a bitter edge. "The upper classes aren't the only ones willing to pay for dragons. We'll hold open auctions. We'll make a fortune. The upper classes will pay big to stop the merchant class from getting their hands on a dragon."

Fen looked at him thoughtfully. "And what's to stop you from taking River from me? I'd be seen as your protégée."

"We'd set it up like a business deal. Listen boy, you won't have a better offer. Where else will you find a stable willing to take you in? Well, take you in without trying to steal your dragon."

"I want a better show of faith. As you keep pointing out, I'm a mere boy compared to you. I have much more to lose since most of my life is still ahead of me. My dragon's my life. I have no other skill to earn a living with."

Hanun tapped his chin. "Hmm. I have no children.

When I die there's no one to inherit all this." Hanun waved to the house they were in. "I'll make a will stating if you live with me for a year and let our dragons breed, you'll inherit on my death, even if you're not living with me at the time."

"And if you die before the year is up? Accidents do happen."

"Then if you're living with me, you automatically inherit." Hanun paused before adding, "As long as I don't die through foul play."

Fen wondered how far he could trust him. "Who's your brother?"

"Adalric Renarlo con Vexartian."

Fen's jaw dropped. He was momentarily speechless.

"What? Don't tell me you're afraid of him. A pox on you if you are. I didn't take you for a coward. Maybe what I took as courage earlier was plain rudeness."

Fen shook his head. "You don't know?"

"Know what?" Hanun rose to his feet.

Fen also stood. "Your brother's the one causing me this trouble. He's the one who most wants my dragon."

Hanun pointed a finger at him. "Name your price, boy. Hell, I'll sign it all over to you tomorrow. I'll sign a blood oath. Name your price. I'll pay it. Help me bring him down and it's all yours."

Fen shook his head, more in bewilderment than denial.

"I haven't more to offer."

Fen held up a hand. "Please. I need a minute. I need time to think."

"You aren't dismissing my offer?"

"No. It's very generous. I'll have to talk to a lawyer and have something written up. I'll get back to you today."

"Whatever you choose. Bring it here. I'll sign it. I'm not having him win again," Hanun stated wildly.

Fen sighed. He wanted to take Hanun's second offer. He wanted to own the man's home, his female dragon, all of it. He could feel the joy of owning his own home and stables burning through him. He pushed that thought away. He was no longer a thief. He'd left that life behind. Besides, if he took everything, how long would it be before Hanun was looking at ways to get even with him? "A partnership."

"A what?"

"I'll buy half your home and stable for a token price. If we're partners I can't be seen as your protégée and you can't claim my dragon. We'll split the profits and both keep ownership of our own dragons. You'll write a final and binding will that cannot be broken leaving the other half of your home and stables to me. I'll leave it up to you what decision you make on who has your dragon on your death."

Hanun stared at him, speechless for a moment. "I handed you a fortune, boy."

"I know."

"Why didn't you take it?"

"Because I'm not Adalric."

There was a moment of silence. Hanun nodded, a smile starting to form. "So you aren't, boy."

"It's Fen."

Hanun held out his hand. "Welcome to Carson Dragon Stables. Fen."

Chapter Eighteen

Edana and Fen sat under a cluster of trees while their horses grazed nearby.

Edana stared at him in silence, her mind trying to sort out all Fen had told her. "I didn't even know I had an uncle. I want to meet him."

"You can't. I've already explained he wants to do everything possible to make your father miserable. And your father feels the same. I bet he'd love to tell Adalric his own daughter visits him."

"I'm sure I could talk him into keeping my secret." There had to be a way. She was certain she could convince him.

"No. We can't risk it. I don't want anyone putting things together and noticing the age of my dragon and the age of the one your father had stolen. I don't know how to lie to a direct question from a truthsayer. Do you want your father to end up with

River? He wants him because he thinks he's wild. If he's a tame grey he'll have no use for him. They're a liability. Do you want to risk your father having him slaughtered for parts?"

"What rubbish." Edana shook her head. How many times did she have to tell him? "Dragon Lords lose grey dragons regularly. It's rare for anyone to raise them. You can't prove ownership. No one would even think their dragon was still alive after this long."

"We aren't going to risk it."

"I want to meet him."

"Not as yourself. I'll think of a way."

"Don't take too long."

"I won't let even you put River at risk."

Edana met Fen's sharp gaze for a moment then looked away. She didn't want to risk River either, but Hanun was her family. "I want to meet him. I want to know him."

"When the time's right."

Edana paused. She could be patient for a while. She nodded. "Fine. I'll hold you to that. But for now, I have to go. I've been out longer than usual."

"Tomorrow morning?"

"I hope so." Edana rose to her feet and untied the reins of her horse. She mounted, waved to Fen and turned her horse towards home. Fen had better hurry up and find a way for her to meet Hanun, or she'd come up with her own plan.

* * *

It was nearly a month before Fen arranged a time for Edana to meet her uncle. During that time, he trained River every day until he was flying steadily and beginning to pick up speed. And also, much to River's delight, Fen had a fireplace and wooden floorboards put in his pen. River and Pearl also mated and Pearl laid four eggs.

The day Fen collected Edana, River started to learn how to do rapid spins and turns in mid flight. Fen was annoyed he had to call him in to leave in time to collect Edana. Even River was reluctant to come in.

Fen met Edana not far from her home. She was dressed in her widow woman's clothes and Fen had brought his old horse for her to ride. Both horses were now stabled at the home he shared with Hanun.

"I don't see why I should have to ride the nag," Edana complained as she mounted the horse. "I'm the better rider out of the two of us."

"I'm surprised you didn't also point out you paid for them, Ed."

Edana looked at him in surprise. "But that was part of our deal. I give you all the money I can to save River."

Fen smiled. "With how River's flying you won't have to keep giving me money to look after him soon."

"Then what am I going to spend it on?"

Fen laughed. "You make it sound like it's going to be a problem."

"It will. With the amount of money I've been getting off my father I can't suddenly stop."

"Then I guess I'll hold onto it for when you leave home."

"I can't. Blood trackers, remember?"

"Do you like being owned by him?"

"It isn't all bad. He doesn't expect too much from me. Not lately, anyway."

"He will."

"How much further until we get to Uncle Hanun's place?"

"Don't call him that."

"He's my uncle."

"He's not to know. Edana! We won't be going if you can't remember to call him Hanun." Fen pulled his horse to a stop.

Edana stopped and looked back at him. "Fine. I'll

remember." When Fen continued to stare at her, she said, "I promise."

He told his horse to walk on. "You're not to call him uncle even in your mind."

"I'm not an idiot. I can remember not to call him uncle."

"I don't want to risk you slipping up. River's too important to risk him like that."

"Fine."

They continued to the Carson Dragon Stables in silence. First Fen took Edana to see River who leaned down to rest his head against hers.

"I've missed you too." Edana rubbed River's neck. "I had no way to come and see you. I'm sorry. It might be a day of rest for most people, but my father's been taking me with him when he attends different functions. I'd rather come and see you."

"What?" Fen asked when Edana laughed.

"He thinks you should organise things better so I can visit more often."

Fen smiled. He rested his hand against River's neck. "I'm sorry. I can't always arrange things to suit what we want. I'll try and get Eddie here more often."

Edana spent a little longer with River until Fen reminded her they'd arranged to have lunch with

Hanun. Edana said goodbye to River and then walked beside Fen, her fingers worrying at her cloak.

Fen reached out to still her hands. "He's nice. A bit gruff, but nice. Well, to most people, anyway." He grinned. Edana's answering smile was strained. "Come on." They walked towards the dining room where they found Hanun waiting for them.

Edana's footsteps slowed as they approached the dining room so she was walking behind Fen when they entered.

"Hanun, I'd like you to meet Yileen. Yileen, this is my partner Hanun." Fen stepped to the side so Hanun could see Edana.

"You didn't tell me she was a widow," Hanun said to Fen as he came forward. "Pleased to meet you, my dear. Sorry for your loss."

"Thank you, but it wasn't recent. The veil was part of a vow I took."

"Surely you shouldn't be held to a vow you made whilst grieving."

"It won't be much longer before I've seen out the terms of my vow."

"Please, be seated." Hanun gestured towards the table.

Once they were seated, servants entered with food.

They served Edana first, moved on to Hanun at the head of the table and then to Fen on his left.

Fen looked across the table at Edana and wondered how she was going to eat with the veil on, but she seemed to have no problem. Wanting to keep the conversation away from her, Fen turned to Hanun. "You should have seen River today. With the way he's doing flying turns and spins, we'll be entering him in events before much longer."

"I'm sure our guest doesn't want to hear about dragons," Hanun said.

Edana laughed. "That was how we met, over dragons."

Fen smiled, meeting Edana's gaze. "We met about the time I saved River. She helped me care for him."

"And I've been very attached to River since I first met him," Edana said.

"How rare. A female from the upper classes who likes dragons," Hanun said.

"What makes you say I'm from the upper classes?"

"Your voice. Royals and nobles have a certain tone to their voice and a way of pronouncing their words no other class has. The boy here has it occasionally, like he was around them a lot. But not all the time, not like you do," Hanun explained.

Edana nodded. "Fen tells me you have a female dragon."

"Ah, yes. My Pearl. She's a beauty. A pure white with silver markings through her wings. You'll have to see her after lunch. She likes it when people admire her."

"I'd appreciate that. My family don't encourage my interest in dragons. They're the most fascinating creatures," Edana said.

"Who are your family?" Hanun asked.

There was silence for a minute before Fen said, "E… Yileen is having problems with her family. It's difficult for her to talk about them."

"Humph! Families. More trouble than they're worth," Hanun grumbled. "I could tell you stories to make you glad you don't have a brother like mine."

"I doubt many people would have as many family problems as you've had, Hanun," Fen said.

"I could've done without a brother to mess up my life," Hanun said.

"I was surprised by how much you look like him," Edana said.

"How do you know my brother, girl?"

"I…" Edana started then turned to Fen.

"Stop trying to terrify our guest, Hanun. I told her who your brother is. I didn't think it was a secret. As you pointed out, she's from the upper classes. Doesn't everyone know each other amongst them?" Fen asked.

"Everyone knows each other and they stick together like burrs. About as annoying as burrs. So, what do you think of my brother?"

"I don't always agree with everything he says, but surely you've been amongst the upper classes. Females are decorative. A show of wealth."

"Like statues you mean," Fen said.

"Absolute waste. I don't know how any of you put up with that," Hanun said.

"We're trapped in it by birth. Some of us escape, some are born to modern parents, and others bear it. My mother's one of those who cheerfully embraces the life. She sees it as a job. She does well with her wooden appearances and my father rewards her with expensive gifts. I've learned to mostly remember my place. Sometimes I forget," Edana said.

"Humph. Don't deserve a child, your parents. You should be free of them since you're widowed. You're welcome to stay here," Hanun said.

"Oh." Again Edana looked towards Fen.

"Well," Hanun asked. "What do you think?"

"It's complicated, Hanun," Fen said. "It involves others than herself. She's caught up in something she can't easily get away from at the moment. Give it time."

"Well, the offer's open. Take it up any time. The boy's a smart one. I doubt he'd call you friend if you weren't deserving of the title. You'd be better company than his stableboy. Has a mouth and a half on him."

Fen smiled. "There's nothing wrong with Mouse. He's as loyal as they come."

"To himself, maybe. Only completely loyal when food's involved," Hanun muttered. "Are you finished eating? Why don't we see my Pearl. She'd love that."

When they nodded, Hanun led the way to Pearl's pen.

* * *

"Oh, she's beautiful." Edana tried to reach forward with her mind like she did with River but encountered something like a solid wall. Not wanting to force herself on the dragon, Edana pulled back, sending a question to River about the wall.

"Only greys can communicate with humans. All other tame dragons are deaf to you," River explained, his words still a little indistinct and hard to understand.

Edana wanted to ask him more, but Hanun was looking at her expectantly. Had he asked her something while she was distracted by River? "Do you think she'd let me pat her?"

Hanun shook his head. "She's not as friendly as River. She's had a hard life. No mate until now and no other dragons to keep her company. Nothing. My brother has a lot to answer for. Hey, old girl?" Hanun looked towards Pearl. "But that'll change soon. You'll have young ones hatching before you know it."

Pearl leaned forward, as if to agree.

The rest of the visit was filled by Fen showing Edana and Hanun River's new flying skills. He loved showing Edana who sent him lots of approval as she watched.

Edana was also able to come to lunch the next three Restdays and Hanun started to expect her.

Chapter Nineteen

Hanun was disappointed when on the fourth Restday Edana was unable to attend. The following Halfday would be River's first event at the competition grounds. He was entered in the novice races.

"Will Edana be there next Halfday?" Hanun asked Fen.

"I don't know," Fen said.

"Then send her an invitation. We can collect her on the way."

Fen shook his head. "She'll be there if she can. Her life's not simple."

"I keep telling her she's welcome here. Why won't she come? You know her story. What's the problem?"

Fen stared at Hanun for a moment, trying to think what to say. "I'm sorry, Hanun. I can't tell you. It's not my story to tell."

"Humph. How convenient. Well, get back to that

dragon of yours. He needs to be ready for Halfday."
Hanun waved Fen away.

Fen nodded and went to see River. He hadn't
realised how difficult living with Hanun would be.
He had to watch everything he said. Hanun picked
up on the slightest slip. He still didn't trust Hanun to
protect Edana's secret when it could further his own
revenge.

Fen and Mouse put River through his paces all
afternoon as well as the rest of the week. Mouse
had been taught the hand movements most trainers
used so their dragons would fly where they wanted
them to. River knew them, but ignored them. It
didn't matter how many mistakes Mouse made. River
listened only to the instructions Fen sent.

The following Halfday they were busy
transporting River to the competition grounds. Too
busy for Hanun to enquire after Edana again. They
had to sign in, find the pen River had been assigned
for the day and make sure Mouse wore the uniform
of Carson Dragon Stables. He was disgusted by the
lack of colour in the mostly black clothes with a few
trims and markings of silver and pearl white. It was
nothing like the colourful clothes he wore every day.

Fen watched from the owner's area as race after
race filled the rest of the morning. Novice races were

after lunch. He took his lunch in the pen with River and talked to him about what was expected. He was far more nervous than River and grateful for the waves of reassurance River sent him.

"Don't see why you bother. Never heard him answer you yet," Mouse grumbled from the corner of the pen. "Dreadful colours." He tugged at his sleeve.

Fen ignored him and shared his sandwich with River. *"Do your best. I don't expect you to place on your first race,"* he thought to River.

"What a waste. I'd have eaten it," Mouse grumbled.

There was a firm knock on the pen door and it opened to admit one of the competition grounds' stablehands. "Time to ready the novices. Their races start shortly." The door closed behind him and they heard him knock on a door several pens away.

Fen turned back to River. "Come on then. Let's show them what we can do."

River followed Fen while Mouse trailed behind and grumbled. They were joined in the corridors by other dragons and trainers. When they reached the race arena doors, they were directed to wait in the cavernous area for those ready for the next race. Outside they heard a round of applause as the race before theirs finished. The doors opened and the official at the door called out the names of the dragons competing.

Finally River's name was called and he and Mouse moved forward. Fen's stomach turned over as he watched them. Today the other Dragon Lords were about to see what his dragon could do. He was nervous and excited.

Fen hurried to the owners' area since he wasn't allowed into the race arena. Only competing dragons and their trainers were. There'd been several arguments between Hanun and Fen over that. Fen didn't trust anyone with River and would have none of the trainers Hanun wanted to arrange. Hanun refused to let Fen be River's trainer. It was unheard of and Hanun was determined Fen would take his place amongst the Dragon Lords. In the end, Fen decided Mouse would be the trainer since he knew Mouse wouldn't be annoyed at the lack of attention River would pay him. Anyone else would notice and comment on how River responded.

Fen reached the owners' area as the race began, dragons with outstretched wings taking to the air. He pictured the race plan they'd been shown when they signed in that morning. He concentrated on reminding River where he had to fly. Owners bumped him as they called out to their own dragons or their favourites. Fen pushed it all from his mind. He showed River the course, bit by bit. He guided him through the rock spires in the middle of the arena that had to be completed in a certain pattern. Then he urged him to the first checkpoint.

"Looks like your dragon's doing well," Adalric said from beside Fen, breaking his concentration.

River faltered. "I'm sorry. I won't be much of a conversationalist at the moment. First race and all." Fen tried to keep River on track while Adalric continued to stand beside him.

"You'll get the hang of it. Before long you won't even notice your dragon flying. You'll be too busy catching up with friends. I hear you've moved to the Carson Dragon Stables. It really isn't a good move. There's much you don't know about the man," Adalric said.

Fen tried desperately to concentrate on River. But he also needed to focus on the conversation. The dragons were drawing close to another round through the spires in the middle. Fen needed all his concentration. "I've been pleased with the way he treats myself and my dragon."

"Who's to know what plans he has for your future. You want to be careful what ulterior motives the man has. You should be wary of a man no Dragon Lord wants to associate with."

The spires in the middle came closer. River was in the lead.

Edana joined them. "Father, I've been looking for you."

Fen sent her a look of relief before he turned back to concentrate on River. He'd lost ground, not knowing which direction to take through the spires. Fen showed him, step by step. They were holding fifth place now. Seven dragons trailed behind them. Edana could've said anything to her father, Fen wouldn't have heard. All his concentration was focused on his dragon. River flew, Mouse directed from below, his movements vaguely corresponding to where River was. Fen barely noticed Adalric's hand as it dropped onto his shoulder. Adalric was distracted by his daughter again.

Fen urged River through the other dragons as he aimed for the last checkpoint. Fen sent picture after picture to River, showing him how the dragons closed in around him. River streaked through them. He avoided one coming in on his left and flew below one coming from the right. He was now in fourth place, the checkpoint nearly upon them. With a last burst of speed, River wove and ducked, passing one more dragon before he flew past the checkpoint. There was a round of applause and Fen held his breath, waiting for the announcement of the three dragons that placed.

Fen was nearly knocked off his feet as Adalric clapped him on the shoulder. "Not bad for a first flight. Not bad at all."

Then came the announcements. "First place to Golden Fancy of Renarlo Dragon Stables, second place to Ruby's Jett of Omanato Dragon Stables and third place to River of Carson Dragon Stables."

"Better luck next time," Adalric said. "Not a bad first flight. Now if you'd been at a stable where decent trainers were available you might have even won. If you change your mind about your present accommodations, let me know. We'd make sure you had a good trainer rather than that sorry looking fellow down there." Adalric pointed towards Mouse who called River to him so they could exit the arena.

"Thank you. Congratulations on first place," Fen replied.

Adalric shrugged. "It's no more than I expected. She's fast, my Golden Fancy. A real streaker. Her mother was the same. Nearly all the offspring of her mother have been fast. I've never seen the like of them before and probably never will again. We lost her mother last year. A pity none of her daughters have passed along that streaker gene. At least the number of greys born to my stable has reduced since she died."

"Father, your guests are waiting."

Adalric gave Edana a warning glare before he turned to Fen. "My guests will be waiting to congratulate me. Come, daughter." Adalric turned and started to walk away without checking to see if Edana followed.

Edana stepped closer to Fen to keep their conversation private. "Tell River I was proud of him."

"He would've done better if I hadn't been distracted by your father."

"It was probably best. No one takes first place the first event they're in."

Fen smiled. "It would've been nice." He paused, his smile fading. "Golden Fancy's ma, was that-"

Edana interrupted. "Yeah. She was River's mother. But Golden Fancy, she's not like River. I don't know why it's only the greys who can talk to people. And I wonder if all the other greys were the same as River. I should've paid more attention to them. Saved them somehow."

"At least you saved River."

Edana nodded. "I'd better go before they wonder where I am."

"Tomorrow morning?"

Edana nodded before she pushed through the crowd.

Fen looked around at the people discussing the next races. He wasn't interested. He wanted to check on River. He threaded his way through the crowd and was nearly barrelled over by Mouse who ran into him as he reached the door that led to the pens.

"Rhone's here and he's seen you," Mouse whispered to Fen.

"I'm heading to River's pen. That'll be a quiet enough place to meet up with him. Keep Hanun busy. I don't want him walking in on us."

"What'll you do?"

Fen stared at him thoughtfully. "I don't know yet. Just keep Hanun busy."

Mouse ran back the way he'd come and Fen made his way to River's pen. Fen let River know he was there without going inside. He didn't want Rhone any closer to River than he needed to be. River assured him he understood.

"So here you are. I could hardly believe my eyes when I saw you out there. You think you're an important man now, don't you?" Rhone sneered. He stopped in front of Fen who turned so he could lean against River's door.

"You saw the race?" Fen asked mildly. He was glad everyone was interested in the rest of the races so the area was deserted.

"I haven't come to discuss some damn race and you know it."

"Possibly you've come to apologise for your treatment of me the day you kicked me out?"

"You deserved every bit of that beating. You failed and I don't tolerate failures. So, where did you hide my dragon? You stole him and passed him off as yours, didn't you?"

"Haven't you heard? He's a wild dragon. Not some tame one you sent me after." Fen kept his tone light.

"Rubbish. I don't believe in coincidences. He's mine."

Anger coursed through Fen, and he struggled to keep it under control. "River's mine. You beat me nearly to death and although it changed my life, I'll never forgive it. You see, I crawled off into the swamp, half dead. A kind person found me and nursed me to health and it was while I was living in the swamp I saved River. I really should be thanking you for the turn my life took, but I can't bring myself to."

"You lie. I'll have a truthsayer find out. You can't lie to them."

"What are you going to tell them? Will you have them ask me if he's the dragon you sent me to steal? How do you think Adalric will take it that you tried to steal one of his dragons? He's an important man." Fen forced himself to relax against the door of River's pen.

"Don't go getting too smart. A quiet word here and there and rumours will run wild."

"So they will. It works both ways, Rhone."

Rhone pointed at him with his walking stick. "I'm not finished with you."

"I didn't think so." Fen smiled, no joy in it. "I look forward to it. We have a score to settle. I believe I owe you a broken rib or two."

"You deserved that you slimy little-"

Rhone's words were cut off as Fen moved swiftly forward, grabbing him by the throat. "I've come a long way since you considered yourself my master. I won't tolerate you talking to me like that. I believe our conversation is over." Fen pushed Rhone roughly from him.

"For today. Only for today," Rhone spat before he stalked off.

Once he was certain Rhone was gone, Fen slipped

into the pen and tried to calm himself. When footsteps sounded outside, River sent him a wave of reassurance.

Hanun entered River's pen. "That boy of yours talks some nonsense."

Fen calmed himself before he turned to Hanun, a smile on his face. "But he did well by us today. Him and River. They brought a third placing to our stables."

"So they did." Hanun's mouth turned into a cheek splitting grin. "I'll have to organise a feast for that boy. He certainly deserves it. Never seen a lad put away as much food as he does." Hanun shook his head in amazement. "So, first next time?"

Fen laughed. "Why not? What do you think, River? First next time?"

River dipped his head and Hanun laughed.

"Anyone'd think he agreed."

"So they would," Fen said softly, amused at how everyone thought dragons no smarter than a horse or dog.

"Have you been up to collect your third place prize money yet?"

"I thought you might like to." Fen didn't want to leave River's side while Rhone was about.

Hanun rubbed his hands together. "That I would.

That I would." He hurried out of the pen, his step brisk, and whistled cheerfully.

Chapter Twenty

"Where are you going?"

Edana spun, a hand still resting on her horse's saddle, the reins also in that hand. "Nowhere, father. Just for a ride."

"Alone?"

"I'm not going far."

"What have I said about riding alone?"

Edana dropped her gaze to the stableyard ground, trying to hide her anger. "That it's not safe."

"And?"

"I'm not to ride alone." Her head rose. "But I'm not going far."

"You." Adalric pointed to a stableboy who hurried to his side. "Unsaddle the horse and put it away."

Edana continued to clutch the reins for a moment before she let the stableboy take her horse. "I wasn't going far," she muttered.

"Take a stableboy with you in future. Now go to your room."

Edana glared at her father's retreating back. She was tempted to saddle another horse and go. She thought of Fen waiting. Her hands tightened into fists. But she couldn't. She momentarily closed her eyes. She had to think of River. Any trouble she caused for Fen would also affect River.

It wasn't fair. Someone must have said something. She looked around the stableyard. It was quiet. Like always. Her father was never at the horse stables at this time of day. Usually he was asleep. The stableboy came out of the stable and with a glance towards her, hurried away.

Had he been the one who'd told her father? Maybe she should try even earlier tomorrow morning. Before anyone thought of waking. Yes, that should work. Holding back a smile, she strode towards her bedroom. He wasn't going to stop her. Mornings were hers. She gave enough of her day to him and the way he thought she should live.

* * *

The next week passed quickly for Fen. Edana didn't

turn up at the Restday lunch, much to Hanun's disappointment. He wanted to share River's triumph with her. She was also absent in the early mornings when Fen normally met her. Instead, Fen spent all his spare moments teaching River to remember complicated flying patterns so if he was distracted again River would still be able to keep going.

Halfday came before they were ready for it. Fen was once again nervous even though he knew what to expect at the competition grounds. The wait through the earlier races seemed to crawl and Fen joined River during lunch. Again he left River at the race arena door after making sure River remembered the flight pattern.

In the owners' area, Fen looked for a spot where he'd be less likely to be disturbed. It was difficult since he now knew so many of the Dragon Lords.

The race began. The dragons flew into the sky as each aimed for first place. River headed for the front of the pack. Fen sent him pictures of where other dragons were compared to him. There was no need for River to look anywhere but ahead. He weaved amongst the other dragons and glided close to the spires in the middle of the arena. Second place. The dragon ahead of him glanced back. The gap closed. Another dragon tried to come past him on his right. River flew towards him. The distance shrank. Fen showed him one coming up on the left. River weaved. The dragon in first looked back again. The gap shortened. The first checkpoint loomed ahead. River gained on the first dragon as they spun and came towards the spires again. River was on the tail of the first dragon. They wove through the spires. Fen sent picture after picture. River glided close to the spires, his wings tucked in so as not to tear them.

The lead dragon glanced back and River shot past her. She tried to come along his left again. River swerved. They were coming to the final checkpoint. The dragon aimed for River's left. The opening closed. She tried to go above him. River shot forward.

A round of applause signalled the end of the race and Fen nearly slumped to the ground from excitement and tension. He held himself still and breathlessly waited for the announcer.

"So this is where you hid." Adalric came up beside him.

Fen glanced over to him, a polite nod for Adalric, another for Edana who stood beside her father.

Adalric turned to see who Fen greeted. "I thought I said for you to stay with our guests."

"Sorry. I didn't hear you." Edana lowered her eyes.

"Didn't hear me? You seem to hear very little of

what doesn't suit you lately." Anything else Adalric might have said was stopped by the announcer.

"Quite a race today. Unexpected results. First place goes to second time racer River of Carson Dragon Stables, second place to Golden Fancy of Renarlo Dragon Stables and third place to Ruby's Jett of Omanato Dragon Stables."

There was a rush of sound from the crowd as everyone talked at once about the newcomer's success.

"Congratulations." Edana broke the silence between Adalric and Fen.

"Not bad," Adalric said grudgingly.

"Thank you," Fen said.

Hanun came through the crowd to stand beside Fen. His eyes fell on his brother, distaste written on his face. He turned to Fen. "Good showing. A lot of potential our River." He stressed the word 'our'.

"Don't expect it always. Wait until he's experienced enough to join the regular events," Adalric said.

"We look forward to it." Hanun glared at his brother.

"Make the most of the novice races while you can. Before you know it, he'll be one of the crowd again. His wonder status reduced amongst experienced racers." Adalric turned to his daughter and said sharply, "Edana." He strode through the crowd, expecting her to follow.

"I'm sorry." Edana stepped closer to Fen. "My father doesn't like to lose. It doesn't happen often."

"Your father," Hanun said.

"You're well?" Fen ignored Hanun.

Edana nodded. "If I can forget the walls have eyes. Very vigilant eyes." A bitter smile and she turned to hurry after her father.

"You want to explain that to me, boy?"

"What?"

"Don't play dumb with me. I can recognise voices no matter the face that goes with them. Or doesn't."

Fen almost groaned. "You speak in riddles, Hanun. Why don't you collect our winnings?"

"This conversation isn't ended. I'll collect the winnings, but we'll deal with this later or I'll ask others the truth of the matter."

Fen nodded. He watched Hanun walk off as he tried to come up with a way to get out of telling Hanun the truth. And if that was impossible, how much of the truth it was safe to tell him. He thought Hanun had grown fond of him and Edana over the weeks, but his hatred for his brother was strong. It had consumed him for decades.

His hatred for his brother… Fen smiled, in mid-thought. His hatred for his brother might be the key. Feeling more confident of his next move, Fen sauntered down to where River was stabled and congratulated him on his flying.

"And what about me?" Mouse demanded.

Fen and River shared a moment of amusement. "Thank you, Mouse. You did a great job."

"Not that it would've mattered."

"What's that supposed to mean?"

Mouse looked Fen straight in the eye. "I'm not stupid."

"I never said you were," Fen hedged.

"I'm out there for show." Mouse pointed towards River. "He don't need me, but it'd be strange to them if he didn't. You just don't want questions."

"Maybe you should remember that."

"There's a blood oath," Mouse complained.

"Sometimes there's ways around them."

"Not if you don't want there to be."

Fen measured Mouse's response. Finally he nodded.

"Do I get another feast for being such a good trainer?"

Fen grinned. "Every night if we keep taking first place."

"You will, won't you?" Mouse asked River. He

turned back to Fen. "It took me a bit, but I figured it out. River's different. I hadn't met other dragons so I didn't know. But I'm not stupid." Mouse glanced behind him. "Someone's coming." He slipped outside.

After the run in with Rhone last time, Mouse had somehow managed to get them a pen at the end of the corridor. Fen was glad. He didn't want to risk River. A pen easily guarded had been welcome. Mouse entered.

"One of Rhone's people. They've gone. They know where I am now." Mouse had paled, his eyes wide.

"Is that a problem?"

"I don't know. He has a blood oath on me too. Don't know what it says though. Didn't think it'd matter. He would have heard I was caught in the market. I reckoned he would have thought me dead."

Fen closed his eyes and tried to calm himself. He could have shaken Mouse. Then he reminded himself of how willing he'd once been to do anything for a feed and a relatively safe place to stay.

"You kicking me out?"

Hearing the fear in Mouse's voice, Fen shook his head and opened his eyes. "No. But, I'll have to think about this. We can't have him calling up an unknown oath on you at the wrong moment."

"What can we do?"

"Give me time. I'll figure it out."

Mouse looked relieved. "I'll get everything ready to take River home."

Fen nodded. He turned back to River as soon as Mouse had gone. "Any brilliant ideas? I sure could use some help."

River sent a wave of reassurance.

Fen sighed. "Thanks, River." He closed his eyes and leaned against River. His hand absently stroked the scales.

Chapter Twenty-One

As soon as River was settled in his pen at the Carson Dragon Stables, Hanun grabbed Fen by the shoulder.

"No escape, boy."

"I wouldn't think of it. I was going to organise a snack for us. It's been a busy afternoon."

"A couple of minutes and then I come looking for you."

Fen smiled. "You'll enjoy this tale, Hanun. We were going to tell you. Just not yet. You're absolutely going to love the plan we're slowly putting into motion."

"I had better." Hanun strode to his sitting room.

Fen quickly arranged for refreshments before he joined Hanun. He also used those minutes to organise what he planned to say. He knew he'd only have one chance to get this right. Hanun wasn't pleased he'd been kept in the dark. Especially since it was something to do with his hated brother.

Fen sat near Hanun and looked out at the paved courtyard. He listened to Hanun's fingers as they drummed on the arm of his chair. He wasn't certain what was the best way to start the story. He needed a way to make Hanun sympathetic to Edana.

"Do you remember what you said the first time Edana dined here?" Fen asked.

"What has that to do with anything?"

"We talked about how females of the upper classes are only there as decoration. A status symbol."

"I'm not senile, boy. I remember."

"Then surely you recall Edana saying she's trapped by her birth. She's been searching to find a way to make her own life. But if you've been amongst the upper classes you should know how tightly they hold onto anything they think is theirs."

"Even if it isn't theirs to hold onto," Hanun said bitterly.

"Exactly. Edana's desperate to escape her father's not so tender care. But she can't. She's trapped."

"How? Surely she could leave any time. You'd take care of her. Hell, she could come here. She's my niece after all."

Fen shook his head. "Far more complicated,

Hanun. She isn't a widow. That's a disguise she uses to escape his notice. He has her birth blood and in the eyes of the law he owns her until she reaches twenty. Now if you know of a way around those two problems, I beg you to tell me."

Hanun shook his head. "Blood's binding."

"So we've found. If her father knew she was coming here, he'd kill her. But she needs to escape sometimes."

"Then why hasn't she been coming lately?"

"You heard her. The walls have eyes. She's been watched more than usual, Hanun. I think her father suspects something. We need to know if you'll help her if possible. I don't know if anyone can help, but…"

"Of course I'd help her. It's not like she asked to have the parents she has. What a family to be born into. Most of them are scum."

"So we can count on your help? And to keep our secret until we can find a way to get Edana away from her father?"

Hanun grinned. "He'll hate to lose her. She's his only heir."

Fen nodded. "He'll turn the country upside down. We've got to find where he's hidden her blood. Then she'll be free."

"Oh, this is too good. Just too good." Hanun leapt to his feet. "Do you have any idea where it might be hidden?"

"We're working on it."

"Is there anything I can do to help find it?"

Fen shook his head. "We're trying not to raise his suspicions. We don't want it hidden too well."

"Hmm. No." Hanun paced the room. "He wouldn't trust it too far from him. He'd want to lay his hands on it in a hurry."

Fen nodded and let Hanun plot and plan.

"Has his study been searched? Maybe a secret panel in the wall or behind a picture? Or a false bottom in a drawer. The study seems the most likely place. He'd want it in an area only he'd go."

Fen calmly nodded when he would have preferred to shout in triumph. Hanun was caught.

"I have to think about this. There has to be some logical place to keep it," Hanun muttered as he walked from the room. He didn't even pay any attention to Fen who was finally able to let his smile break free.

* * *

Fen was relieved to see Edana waiting for him the next day to take her to lunch with Hanun. As soon as they were riding towards Hanun's, Fen told Edana about Hanun's discoveries and what he'd told him.

"But we aren't doing anything of the sort," Edana protested.

"He doesn't have to know that. Besides, if you had a way to escape and not have blood trackers find you, you'd take it."

"Yes, but-"

"Ed, forget it. Stick to my story. As far as Hanun's concerned, you've searched for the blood your father keeps to track you. Listen to his suggestions. If you think they aren't good, say you've searched in those places. Play along."

"I know where it's kept and it's impossible to get. It's locked and spelled so no one but my mother or father can get it."

"Hanun doesn't know that. Let him think you don't have a clue where it is. That you're looking for it."

"I guess I don't have a choice." Edana sighed heavily. "This is all getting so complicated."

Fen smiled. "Surely you hadn't thought it'd be easy."

"I guess not." Edana sighed again. "Oh, I brought a gift for River for doing so well in the races."

"What is it?"

"You'll have to wait and see."

Nothing Fen said could make her tell him and they finally reached Carson Dragon Stables where they went to see River first.

"Oh, you sweet thing." Edana threw her arms around River's neck when he bent his head down to her. "How I've missed you." She buried her face against his scales for a few moments before she pulled away. "I have a present for you." She reached inside her belt pouch and pulled out a small cloth bag.

River bent forward and nosed at the cloth. He lifted one paw and held it out. Edana pulled open the drawstring of the bag and tipped it up. A large ruby fell onto River's paw. His claws closed over it.

"I guess you like it, huh?" Edana asked.

"I like it. Thank you," River thought to her.

"Oh wow. I know Fen said you're getting better at talking, but you're doing it so clearly now," Edana said.

"Quietly," Fen warned.

"Oh, of course. But it's so exciting."

"And he'll be able to speak like us eventually."

"How do you know?"

"He told me."

Edana turned back to River. "I can't wait."

Fen reached out and rested his hand on Edana's shoulder. "We should see Hanun. We need to know where you stand with him."

"Go now," River urged them.

"I wish I had more time to spend with you." Edana said. River lowered his head in acknowledgement. "I'll have to see you fly before I go home today."

"Come on. We need to deal with this," Fen said.

"I'm coming." Edana rested her head for a moment against River.

Hanun waited for them in the dining room. He rose to greet Edana who'd removed her widow's robes.

"Fen told me you're looking to escape your father. Is that the truth?"

Edana stopped, startled by the abrupt question. "Do I seem like the type who enjoys being a decoration? I've dined with you, talked with you. What sort of person do you think I am? One to willingly let another choose their path for them or one who likes to tread her own road?"

Hanun chuckled. "The curse of the family. Good to

see it doesn't skip the females. Come and eat." Hanun sat down.

Fen and Edana sat in their usual seats, one on each side of Hanun.

"I guess you've been and fussed over River. Everyone pays their respects to him first. I should feel jealous of that dragon. Except I'm too pleased with him at the moment. He's something special. Taking first place when he's not much older than two," Hanun said.

"He did well yesterday." Edana moved her hand from the table so a servant could put a filled plate in front of her. "I'm very proud of him so I can imagine how pleased the two of you are."

"How did your father take it? What did he say once he was out of the public eye?" Hanun asked.

Edana laughed. "I see now why you were so pleased to see me today. I'm in the perfect place to tell you how your scheming is affecting the one you're aiming it at."

"Well girl, don't keep me in suspense."

"He was livid. All the servants stayed out of his way and dinner was dreadful. I thought he'd choke on every mouthful. He muttered about beginners' luck, he threatened to fire useless trainers. I've never seen him so angry. He's lost occasionally to Bastian, but never to anyone else. They have the two most successful stables. I think everyone breathes a sigh of relief when they don't have dragons for certain classes or events."

"Good." Hanun raised his glass in a toast. "You've made my year, girl."

"I'm pleased, Uncle Hanun."

Hanun paused, his glass halfway to his mouth. He stared at Edana and carefully placed his glass on the table. He nodded. "So I am." He smiled. "So I am. Well, you're more pleasing a relative than your father. Haven't seen any of him in you yet."

"Oh, there's far too much of him in me," Edana said.

"Her pig-headedness for starters," Fen pointed out.

Hanun stared at Edana for a moment. "For certain. Ah well, at least it's in a prettier package."

The rest of the meal passed pleasantly, finishing with Hanun's suggestions of where to look for Edana's blood. Hanun even suggested bringing in a blood tracker to track it down. Afterwards, they watched River practise. Fen was feeling good on his trip back to Hanun's after delivering Edana to where she'd left her horse. Things were going well. There were still a few difficulties. But on the whole it was going well.

Chapter Twenty-Two

"Didn't I tell you not to ride alone?"

Edana spun to face her father in the dimly lit stable, her horse still in the stall. "I was visiting my horse." It had been a week since she'd managed to find the stable empty. It looked like it hadn't been this time either.

"Don't lie to me. You've been watched. Now where have you been going?"

Edana looked past her father to the stableboy she'd seen the first time her father had caught her. "By him?" She gestured towards the stableboy.

"Who doesn't matter. Where have you been?"

She tried to think of an excuse. It wasn't like she could tell him she was going to spend the day with his brother and Fen. She tried to think of something he'd accept. She drew a blank. "Why don't you ask him?" She pointed at the stableboy. "He seems to know everything."

"I'm asking you. And I'm not going to ask again. Where have you been going?"

"Riding. I'm surrounded by people. Servants. Tutors. I just want some time alone." Her father remained silent as he stared at her and Edana bit back the urge to keep speaking.

"You want time alone."

She hesitated. She didn't like the tone he used. "Yes." Her voice was uncertain.

"Go to your room."

Relief washed over her. That was nothing new. She nodded and walked past her father. The relief evaporated when he fell into step beside her. Should she ask him what he wanted? Did she really want to know? "I can find my own way to my room."

Adalric didn't answer her, striding silently beside her.

She was tempted to try again, but thought it best to remain quiet. When they reached her room, she stopped in the doorway, staring at her father. Eventually she asked, "How long do I have to stay in here?"

"Until I organise your betrothal." Adalric closed the door.

Edana's mouth dropped open as she listened to her door being locked and her father start to walk away. "What?" No answer. "No." She pounded her fists against the wooden door. "Father." Still no answer. "Let me out." She kept pounding and didn't stop until she heard footsteps pass her door without even slowing. She sank to the floor, her back against the door. This wasn't happening. She had to find a way out.

Scrambling to her feet, she hurried to the doors leading onto her balcony and flung them open. She looked over the edge, trying to judge if she could make it to the ground. He wasn't locking her up. No way was he going to marry her off to someone who'd expect her to behave like her mother. She didn't know how she was going to stop him, but she couldn't bear a life of that.

Her bedroom door opening had her spinning to see her father and his wizard in the doorway. She clutched at the rail behind her.

"Inside. Now." Adalric strode towards her when she didn't move.

Edana tried to pull away from him, but it was impossible. "I'm not getting married. You can't make me."

"You'll be betrothed by your seventeenth birthday.

Married within the year." Adalric dragged her into the bedroom before his gaze went to the wizard. "Start the spell."

Edana continued to struggle. "What spell?"

"To keep you in here."

"No." She fought against the hands that held her. When the chanting of the wizard stopped, she was released. She ran towards her open bedroom door. It was like she slammed against an invisible wall. "No," she screamed, turning to face her father. "Don't do this to me."

"I obviously gave you too much freedom. Your mother said I was spoiling you. It stops now. You will act the lady you're supposed to be." Adalric strode from the room, his wizard at his heels.

"Father. Please." She watched as her door was swung shut, leaving her alone. She stared at the timber a moment before she tried to open it. The door wouldn't budge. She screamed in frustration and headed for the balcony doors that were still open. The invisible barrier stopped her from stepping out of the room. She slammed her hand against the barrier, cursing when pain travelled through her hand and arm.

Another scream. It didn't make her feel any better. Anger, fear and determination filled her. River! She'd call River. She tried to reach out with her mind. Nothing. She was completely trapped in her room. Alone and trapped. And it was less than four weeks until her seventeenth birthday.

*　*　*

Fen began to wonder how well things were going when three weeks passed without seeing or hearing from Edana. He hadn't seen her since he and Hanun had dined with her for the first time without her widow robes. The only time without her widow robes. He couldn't help worrying about her.

The only good news during the past three weeks was that Pearl's four eggs were thriving. Keeping an eye on the eggs didn't stop him from wondering what had happened to Edana, especially since he hadn't even seen her at the races on Halfday. He kept reminding himself she'd call for help through River if she was in danger. He had other things to deal with. In particular four thieves had tried to break in during the past three weeks. Each one River had dealt with.

Although Fen hoped the message would get out that wild dragons weren't worth the trouble of trying to steal, he had to deliver his own message. He knew one of the thieves had been from Rhone. The others might have been. He didn't know for sure. There was also the matter of Mouse's blood oath Rhone held. They couldn't hope to keep Rhone away from Mouse forever. Eventually Rhone or one of his people would get a message to Mouse and he'd be forced to carry out Rhone's orders.

First Fen went to River to let him know what he was going to do. When he heard, Mouse begged Fen to stay away from Rhone.

"He's evil," Mouse warned.

"I can deal with him."

"Not on his turf."

"I have to do this."

"I will be there," River told Fen.

"You'll stay away from there," Fen told River.

"Just like you should," Mouse said. "And I wish you'd stop talking to River. It gives me the creeps."

"Rhone has to be dealt with. If I let him walk all over me I'm inviting every criminal to try their hand at stealing from me."

"No you're not. They'll soon get the message River's not to be messed with."

"I'm going with you," River stated firmly.

"River," Fen growled. "You aren't listening."

"Neither are you." River was amused.

Mouse rolled his eyes. "No one's listening." He shrugged. "Well, you might want to find my blood oath while you're there."

Fen looked over his shoulder at Mouse. "I was planning to. Are there any other little surprises I need to know about?"

Mouse shook his head. "Nope. Just that one. It weren't like I wanted to sign it. Was a couple of years after I first joined him. After you left he made all of us sign them."

"Do you know where he keeps it?"

"Not a clue. But you should be able to figure it out."

Fen sighed heavily. "Leave me to it, Mouse. I've got things to sort out."

"I am coming," River reminded him.

"You can't expect to go waltzing in and be welcomed," Fen said to River.

"I will wait on the rooftop. You may tell him I am there. I will tear the house apart if I need to. He is not to lay a hand on you again," River said.

"Fine. But you stay on the rooftop," Fen said.

"As long as he keeps his hands to himself," River said.

"I'll be back shortly. These aren't the clothes for slipping through shadows." As Fen left the pen, he heard Mouse speak to River.

"Don't go letting him get himself killed. He's not too bad you know. And Rhone, he's just evil."

Fen dressed in dark clothes and pulled on a pair of soft-soled boots. He arranged for his horse to be saddled and then returned to let River out. Mouse was no longer in the pen. They made their way outside where Hanun waited for them.

"Want to tell me what you're planning, boy?"

Fen wished sometimes Hanun's servants didn't have to tell him everything. "I'm taking River for a night flight."

"Try again. This time try something I might swallow," Hanun said dryly.

"I have things to deal with."

"Things?"

"Let's just say I've found out who's been trying to steal River. They should give up after tonight."

Hanun nodded. "Always good to stand your ground. Attack is preferable to uncertain defence. Take care." He walked inside, leaving Fen, River and the servant who held the reins of Fen's horse.

Chapter Twenty-Three

Fen took the reins, nodded in thanks and swung into the saddle. He sent an image of the place he was going to and River rose into the air. Fen urged his horse forward. He reminded himself he was now his own man. Rhone wasn't his master and he'd faced him at the competition grounds without a problem. But it had been neutral territory. Fen forced that thought from his mind. He felt the comforting presence of River.

Determination rushed through him. He owed Rhone. It didn't have to be in the same coin. As long as he felt the pain of paying it. Fen reached Rhone's place and rode past. He tied his horse at a tavern down the road and walked back. River let him know he was there. Waiting. Ready to protect.

Fen didn't bother to knock. He flung the door open. A boy, huddled inside, yelped. The boy stumbled to his feet when he saw Fen and raced upstairs. Fen hoped he was going to fetch Rhone. He slammed the door shut behind him and came in as if he owned the place. Act how you want to be treated, he reminded himself.

"Get out!" Rhone yelled from the top of a flight of stairs leading to the next level.

"You have something I want. I have something you want. Only one of us will be satisfied at the end of this meeting," Fen said.

"I haven't time for your nonsense." Rhone moved down the steps. His walking stick tapped on each step as he came.

The sound had once struck fear in Fen. Now it annoyed him. Annoyed him because he knew Rhone did it deliberately.

Rhone smiled, one of pure malice. "I'd have thought you were smarter than to come in here alone. This is my ground. I own everyone in here and they live to serve me." Rhone stopped before Fen.

Fen grabbed hold of the walking stick and slammed it hard against the rails of the steps. It snapped in two. One half flew across the room. Fen threw the other half in the opposite direction. "I'm not a fool. Don't expect me to act one."

Rhone growled, "What am I to think, you coming in here alone."

"I'm not alone." Fen smiled. "You might even say I come with my own army."

Rhone looked around. "I see no one."

Fen glanced up and noticed Rhone did the same. "Oh, my army would tear through the roof to help me if he thought I needed it. You'd be surprised at how quickly my dragon can move. Or maybe you wouldn't. You've seen him take first place the past four weeks. I don't need to tell you how attached he is to me. I'm sure your thieves have come home battered enough for you to see with your own eyes."

"I've sent no thieves."

Fen smiled. Or at least his mouth moved in the shape of a smile. His eyes continued to shoot daggers. "I've already told you not to take me for a fool. I expect two things of you. One, leave us alone. Two, Mouse's blood oath."

"That's not how you make bargains."

"I'm not bargaining. I'm telling you."

"No one tells me what to do. And not in my own place."

"You have to the count of ten to agree. After that, my dragon tears your roof apart," Fen warned. *"You hear me River?"*

"Clearly."

"I'm not falling for that," Rhone said.

"One."

"I have no proof your dragon's here."

"Two. Go look for yourself. But I won't stop counting. Three."

"I should've killed you when I had the chance."

"Four. Yes, that was a mistake. Five. Six."

Rhone glanced up nervously. "Surely we can come to a beneficial agreement."

"Seven. Eight. Not interested. All or nothing."

"I took you in, cared for you, taught you how to survive."

"Nine. Beat me. Starved me. T–"

"Yes! All right. I'll give you the damn oath." Rhone spun on his heel and marched up the stairs.

Fen followed closely. He watched for any tricks or surprises.

"No roof tearing?"

"We wait. It still might happen," Fen told River.

Rhone stopped when he reached his door. "You can't come in here. There's all sorts of private stuff."

Fen looked upwards. "Me or my dragon? Who do you want in there with you?"

Rhone swore, threw his door open and stomped across the room. Fen watched as he opened a panel in the wall and searched through several parchments. He flung one at Fen, who stood there.

"Have you no manners? I've come across wild animals more civilised," Fen said mildly. Than more harshly. "You stretch my patience. Pick it up. Hand it to me."

Rhone glared at him. A sudden scratching on the roof made him look up. Knowing it was River, Fen continued to watch Rhone. The scratching increased and Rhone hurriedly picked up the parchment and handed it to Fen. He read it over and when he saw it was Mouse's blood oath, tucked it in his belt pouch.

"River, can you help me? Can you tell if he has any more of these I need? Anything of Mouse's or even mine?" Fen asked.

"Ask him."

"Now, is there anything else belonging to Mouse? Blood oaths? Blood for tracking? Anything at all?" Fen asked.

"Of course not," Rhone mumbled.

"Lies."

"Try again. This time, tell me what you still have."

Rhone look startled. "You didn't ask for anything else."

"Now," Fen demanded. The scratching on the roof started again.

"You won't always have that dragon around," Rhone muttered. He moved back to the cavity in the wall and searched through everything.

Fen moved forward. He grabbed the sheet off the bed and turned it into a sack. Pushing Rhone out of the way, he scooped everything into the temporary sack.

"You can't do that."

"I'm sick of your lies and deceit. I can do this. Now, do you have anything of mine?"

"No. I wish I did and then you'd regret this."

"True."

"It must be the first truth I've heard out of you all night."

"Get out of here. If you're ever alone watch your back."

"If I come to a nasty end, my dragon will use you to avenge himself. He won't care if you're behind it. And any more of your thieves come our way and the same goes. We're not playing nice anymore. Pass the word around. We'll track the thief to his lair and whoever sent him will wish they were dead. Even a healer wizard won't be able to help. I'm sure you've heard how impossible it is to heal serious wounds made from wild dragon's claws." Fen didn't know if it was true, but the people he was dealing with wouldn't know for certain either.

"I'll stay out of your grounds, you stay out of mine."

Fen nodded. "Sounds fair to me. And that includes anyone I wish to involve myself with. If they're part of my life, even slightly, you stay away from them. I don't care how unimportant they are to me, I'll take it as a personal insult if you interfere." Fen strode from the room before Rhone could reply and went down the stairs. As he headed for the door, he asked River to collect the makeshift bag from him.

River swooped down and took it from his hands as he stepped out the door. Moments later, Fen collected his horse from the tavern and headed home. River flew overhead, watching him.

* * *

Edana scrambled off her bed when she heard the key in her door, letting the book she'd been reading fall closed onto the bedspread. She wondered who'd be at her door at such a late hour.

Adalric swung the door open, dressed as if he'd

been to a social event. "It's been arranged. I've just returned from completing the details."

"Arranged?"

"Your betrothal."

"No." Edana hurried across the room to stand in front of her father. "Please. Don't do this to me. I'm too young to marry. Wait a while. Please."

Adalric shook his head. "It's been arranged. Don't you even want to know who your husband will be?"

"When? When's the betrothal to be signed?"

"Eleven days. Your fiancé and his family will join us here. Once it's been signed you can leave your room."

Hope leapt in her. "I can?"

"The betrothal will be blood oath binding. You can't break it. You'll have to go through with it."

Hope died instantly. "Please. Please don't do this. Father–"

"Enough." Adalric made a sharp motion with his hand. "You will not behave like this when your fiancé and his family arrive. If you embarrass me like this you'll remain in your room." He was silent a moment. "Understand?"

Edana nodded. Words beyond her. Her throat ached and her eyes blinked rapidly.

"You're to be betrothed to Maddov Byram Gratian

con Veseylee. I'll expect you to treat him with respect and act a lady."

She nodded again.

Adalric stared at her a moment longer before he stepped back and closed the door.

It wasn't until she heard her door lock and her father retreating that Edana could move. She sank to the ground where she stood, fighting against the tears that welled. Again she tried to reach out to River. The spell wouldn't let her get past it.

She closed her eyes, covering her face with her hands. Typical that her father would choose the fourth largest dragon stable. If the second and third largest had sons she guessed he'd have chosen them for her to marry into. A half laugh, half sob broke free. Once again she'd messed with his plans by not being a son.

Staggering to her feet, she crossed her room to open the balcony doors. She stared at the star studded night as she pressed her hand against the invisible barrier. Sharp needles of pain shot through her skin. She pressed harder. It made no difference. She was trapped. For another eleven days.

Then she'd be trapped for life.

Chapter Twenty-Four

Over breakfast the next morning, Hanun asked, "Did you deal with your business last night?"

Fen nodded. "We'll have no more problems."

"Humph. There's always other thieves."

Fen smiled slightly. "There'll be no more problems."

Hanun stopped, food halfway to his mouth. He placed the food on his plate and stared at Fen. "Do I ask how you achieved this marvel?"

Fen shook his head. "It's probably best not to. Let's just say I went to the top of the food chain. The message will trickle down. If the top of the food chain is wary, the bottom will be more so."

Hanun nodded. "I always knew you were interesting. I just hope your contacts don't trip you up in life."

"They're more wary onlookers than anyone I'd

associate with. They'll keep at an even greater distance now."

"That's good. Have you heard from Edana?"

"No, but sometimes it's difficult for her to get away."

"You don't think she was caught looking through Adalric's study, do you?" Hanun looked worried.

Fen shook his head. "No. I'd have heard if something drastic had happened."

"I hope so. She's a nice girl. He doesn't deserve to have a child like her."

"He doesn't think so. He's disappointed she's a girl rather than a boy."

"Snake. He doesn't deserve any children."

Fen tried not to smile at Hanun's defence of his niece. He was glad Hanun didn't see her only as a means to get back at his brother. "I need to finish up with some business matters." Fen rose to his feet.

Hanun raised his brows. "Anything I should be concerned with?"

Fen shook his head. "Some loose ends. Ensuring possible future favours."

Hanun nodded solemnly. "Always good to have."

Fen made his way to River's pen and sat on the stool in front of the fireplace. He picked up another one of the parchments he'd taken from Rhone. When Mouse came in and saw him he groaned.

Mouse dropped to the floor. "No more."

"Anything to report?"

Mouse had been returning blood oaths on and off all night for Fen. "The usual. People are happy. Real happy. They all say you can call on them if you need anything."

Fen nodded. "I've got another half a dozen ready." He waved towards the pile. He quickly showed Mouse which oath belonged to which person. "A good thing Rhone put the exact details of each oath on these so we know who to return them to. But I guess there's too many of them to recall all the details otherwise."

As Mouse couldn't read, he tucked each parchment in a different place amongst his clothes. "I might manage to drag myself back."

"You can rest after that lot and deliver some more tomorrow."

Mouse left, muttering under his breath.

"He is not really unhappy," River told Fen.

"I know," Fen smiled. "He wants me to think he is."

It took a bit more than a week for Fen to sort through the parchments. He didn't see or hear from

Edana even once. He started to worry. She'd never been so long without seeing him. He didn't even see her at the competition grounds on Halfday.

Fen leaned against River, the evening quiet around them. "See if you can reach Edana. I know she said it's not good to startle her, but I have to know what's happening."

River was silent a while. *"I cannot reach her. She is in her room but it is spelled."*

"What do you mean?"

"A spell to keep magic out and her from escaping."

"We have to do something. We've got to see if there's some way to climb up to her room or something," Fen said.

"I'll take you."

"How?"

"On my back. Watch my wings. Be careful not to tear them. Sit in front of them. Wrap a rope around my neck but tie it loose. Use it to hold on."

"That won't hurt you?" Fen asked.

A wave of amusement rolled over Fen. *"I am a dragon. You are little more than an insect on a twig to me."*

Fen laughed. "I guess so. Give me a minute. I'll find a rope."

Fen was back minutes later and tied the rope around River's neck. They made their way to the practice arena where Fen climbed on River. Within minutes they were airborne and Fen held tightly to the rope. Once he was over the initial rush of fear, he began to enjoy the ride. The town was spread out below. It was little more than a dark blur dotted with light.

When they reached the Renarlo Dragon Stables, River flew around several times until he found where he wanted to land. He dropped softly onto the roof. His head high as he searched the shadows to check they hadn't been seen.

"Slide over the edge of the roof and you can drop onto Edana's balcony. Do not go in. She can open her door and talk to you, but cannot come out."

"How will that help?"

"See what she needs help with first."

"You're right. I'll see what's wrong." Fen dropped to his stomach and lowered himself over the edge of the roof. He couldn't see below, but he trusted River's directions. He let go and dropped over the edge, landing with a jolt, his knees bent to absorb the impact.

Chapter Twenty-Five

"Edana." Fen raised his voice a bit. He didn't want to call out too loud. "Edana." He waited impatiently. "Edana. At your balcony door."

The curtain at the balcony doors was drawn back. Edana stood there. She glanced over her shoulder then looked towards Fen again.

"Open the door," Fen said.

Edana opened the door. "Are you real?"

"Of course I'm real. What else would I be?" Fen demanded.

"An apparition. Some magic spell created to trip me up," Edana said.

"I'm real."

"How do I know you're real? Prove it."

Fen sighed. "How am I meant to do that?"

"Tell me something only you and I would know."

Fen was silent a moment. "We were brought

together by a dragon and a blood oath." When Edana still looked uncertain, Fen said, "After I suffered a beating for you the least you can do is believe in me when I visit."

"Oh thank the gods of Kalla. You can't imagine how much I've needed you here."

"What happened?" Fen demanded. He was about to step forward when he remembered River had warned him not to.

"My life's over. I'm going to end up a living statue like my mother," Edana wailed.

"Tell me what happened. How can I help if you don't tell me?"

"No one can help me." Edana shook her head as tears pooled in her eyes.

"Try me."

Edana sighed. "It'll be a waste of time. Talk to me instead. I want to know what you and River have been doing. I'll never see you again. How did you get here? Is River well?"

"I am well. How may we help you?"

Fen repeated River's comment since he was unable to send his thoughts through the magical barrier.

"River? Where is he?" Edana asked.

Fen pointed upwards. "He brought me here. I'm sure he can carry you too."

Edana shook her head. "Have you forgotten? Blood trackers. My birth blood is locked away with a spell. And I can't leave here. I've tried. There might as well be a solid wall between you and me. I can't get through."

"What happened? Why are you in here?"

"My father found out I was disappearing. When I wouldn't tell him where I went he decided to betroth me to a Dragon Lord's son. In three days time. On my seventeenth birthday. A betrothal's as binding as a blood oath."

"Then we have to get you out of here," Fen said.

"Haven't you been listening? I can't. Blood trackers and this spell."

"There has to be a way out of this mess. Surely they can't keep you in here always." Fen looked around desperately.

"Only for the next three days. But then it'll be too late. My agreement will be taken and the blood oath given in my name by my father. A wizard can make it binding because by law my father can speak for me," Edana said.

"That's wrong. There has to be some way around it."

"There is."

Fen repeated River's words.

"Impossible," Edana argued.

"Nothing is impossible. All I need is your oath to never reveal my secrets."

"Yes. Of course. I'd be willing to say or do anything to get out of this wedding," Edana promised when Fen told her River's words.

"Your oath that you will not give away my secrets. Freely given with no strings attached."

"Yes," Edana said solemnly when Fen explained.

"Yes. I keep your secrets already," Fen said.

"Then quickly pack what you wish to take. I will explain when we leave here."

Edana stood framed in the doorway a moment longer after Fen had given her River's message. With a single nod she came to a decision. She turned and rushed around her room, gathered items and stuffed them into a couple of bags. That done, she came back to the doorway.

"Now what?" Edana asked.

"Fen. Take your hand and reach out for Edana. Take her by the hand and pull her out of her room. Edana. Relax. Do not try and help. Let Fen pull you through."

Fen explained before he reached forward. His whole arm felt like a million stinging insects were attacking all at once. Ignoring them, he took Edana's hand she held out. He pulled her forward and she yelped. She tried to pull back

"Relax. It cannot harm you. You will be fine in seconds."

"I heard him," Edana exclaimed as she relaxed. She let Fen pull her through onto the balcony. "I'm out. I'm finally out."

A dragon paw reached over the edge of the roof. *"Quickly take hold and let me pull you up."*

They could hear shouting from inside the house. Edana reached out and took hold of River's paw and let him pull her onto the roof along with the bags she held. River's paw appeared again and this time Fen was pulled onto the roof. He disappeared just in time. Edana's door was flung open and Adalric strode in with one of his servants. They heard him bellow Edana's name while they waited on the roof.

He strode onto the balcony. Turning back to the room he called to his servant. "Fetch a blood tracker. She won't be far. She shouldn't have been able to get out of here at all. Wait till I get my hands on that useless wizard."

The moment Adalric had gone inside, Fen and Edana stood up.

"Hop on. We must leave."

Fen showed Edana how to climb on and clambered

up behind her. He put his arms around her waist so he could hold onto the rope since Edana held her bags. As soon as they were ready, River took off. Edana squealed at the sudden movement.

"This is amazing," Edana yelled after several minutes.

"I know," Fen replied, his mouth near her ear.

It seemed like no time before River landed and asked them to hop off. They were along the river not far from the cottage where Fen had raised River.

"What now? They can still send blood trackers." Edana dropped her bags to the ground.

"They will send them after you. But they will not find you. Do you swear on your own life never to reveal this secret I shall share with you? It will be as binding an oath as that of a blood oath given before a wizard."

"Yes," Edana replied.

When River turned towards him, Fen also answered, "Yes."

"Fen, take a knife and make a cut on Edana's hand. Shallow and small will be fine."

"What? No!" Edana drew her hands behind her back.

"This or the wedding."

Edana looked worriedly between Fen and River. She reluctantly held out her hand.

Fen held her hand firmly with his left, the knife poised above it in his right. "Don't move or the cut will be worse."

Edana closed her eyes. "Hurry up and get it over with. A nick is bad enough. But a cut sounds painful."

"It will not be painful for long."

Fen ran the knife across Edana's palm and ignored her sudden gasp. He watched the dark stain appear. In the dim moonlight the colour couldn't be seen.

River moved closer. He held out both his paws. One was above Edana's hand, the other, claws out, was beside it. *"Do not let her move her hand. It will be a fight,"* River said to Fen.

"I'm ready," Fen said.

"I'm not. I don't even know what you're planning," Edana protested.

There was a sudden blur of movement and River used his own claw to cut through the thinner skin between his paw and the start of his leg scales. There was a shimmer of light and then a drop of blood.

Edana screamed as it hit her open cut. "It's burning."

She tried to pull away but Fen wouldn't let her.

Another drop descended and Edana tried to fight Fen. She pulled with her captured hand, her other tried to push him away, her nails scratched at him in her desperation to escape. Another drop hit her palm and she renewed her efforts.

"You're killing me," she half screamed, half sobbed.

Another drop of blood descended and then River licked his paw, the gash seeming to seal. He bent forward and licked Edana's palm and her wound also sealed.

"She can move her hand now," River told Fen.

He slowly released his hold on her and let her gently drop to the ground. Edana held her palm against her chest and sobbed. Fen knelt beside her and tried to hold her in comfort. She pushed at him. A shudder went through her body and she screamed again. Fen's arms went round her and he drew her close.

"What did you do to her?" Fen demanded.

"She will be fine. In a few moments she will be exhausted, but out of pain," River explained.

"Tell us both what you've done." Fen flinched as Edana's body convulsed. He tightened his grip on her. Minutes later she seemed to relax, then went limp as if her body had no bones in it. "River."

"A grey dragon cannot be tracked. My blood has mixed with hers. She now cannot be tracked with her old blood. It has been altered."

"I'm safe?" Edana whispered.

"As safe as any human is."

"I need to sleep." Edana yawned.

"How are we to get her home? She can't hold on while she's this exhausted," Fen said.

"Lay her stretched out flat on the ground. Gather her bags and climb on. I will take you home."

Fen did as River told him, still worried about Edana. He trusted River to tell him the truth, but he was worried River had misjudged the amount of blood or something.

As River took to the air, he gently grabbed Edana in his front paws and let her hang limply in the air as they flew back to the training area of Carson Dragon Stables. He landed gently, careful with how he laid Edana on the ground. Fen slid off River's back and dropped the bags as he rushed to where Edana lay.

He looked back at River. "She's not moving."

"She will sleep deep and long. She will wake for lunch. Make sure there is much for her to eat. She will be starving."

Fen lifted Edana and carried her out of the training area. He strode towards the house and the weight of her seemed to grow greater the longer he carried her. He had to put her down to open the door, but he didn't want too many people to know she was there. After he'd caught his breath, he lifted her again.

Soon he had Edana in one of the guest bedrooms. He laid her in the bed and pulled more blankets from a trunk at the foot of the bed. He didn't think he could move Edana again to get at the blankets she now lay on. Once she was covered, he fetched her bags. He found them at the back door he had entered the house by.

"River?" Fen sent his thought out.

"I have returned to my pen. Sleep well."

"Thank you," Fen thought to River.

"I owe you both my life."

"I owe you as much," Fen thought back.

When River didn't reply, Fen gathered Edana's bags and took them to the guest room. As he stepped out of the guest room and shut the door, a noise behind him made him spin to face it.

"Anything you should be telling me?" Hanun asked.

"Not a thing. But if your brother should come knocking on your door, tell him you haven't seen your niece."

Hanun chuckled. "Oh, this I have to see. What a coup. How fitting."

"Don't you go pestering our guest tomorrow. She'll probably wake late. It's been an exhausting night."

Hanun continued to grin. "You tell our guest she may stay as long as she likes. I hope he does come." He rubbed his hands together. "I don't suppose you're going to tell me what happened."

"Not all of it. But I can tell you the blood trackers can't find her now and she's managed to escape before a betrothal was signed."

"Even better."

Fen looked at Hanun sternly. "I hope you're not going to go on like that around our guest. I'm sure she'd like to think she was here more for her company than her ability to further your revenge."

"Of course not. Not a peep when she wakes. But I can celebrate tonight." With that, Hanun went whistling down the corridor.

Fen slumped against the wall. It seemed like a long way to his room. He sighed and gathered together his last bit of energy. Leaning against the wall wouldn't get him there any sooner.

Chapter Twenty-Six

By the time Edana woke, Adalric had already been and bellowed on their doorstep and demanded to know where his daughter was. He'd found out about her visits and had run out of other places to look. He left after issuing numerous threats.

"How are you feeling?" Hanun asked Edana as she joined them at the table for lunch.

"Like I slept for a year. I hope you don't mind me staying here."

"Of course not. That man who calls himself your father was here earlier. Humph. Throwing his weight around and carrying on."

"I didn't mean to bring trouble to your door," Edana said.

Hanun shook his head. "It's been there since my birth. Enough of this. How is River? Ready for the Halfday races? They're going to be big. There's some out of town dragons entered in the experienced races held in the morning. Everyone will be there to see who takes first in their events."

"What is everyone saying? Has anyone seen them race before?" Fen asked.

"There's going to be a lot betting on them to win from the talk," Hanun said.

"That must be why my father's been angrier than usual. He doesn't like to lose. He also doesn't like it when people think he might lose."

There was noise outside, what sounded like a fight, before the dining room door was flung open. Hanun and Fen had risen to their feet at the first sound. Edana rose to her feet when she saw her father burst into the room.

"I knew it," Adalric bellowed. "Return my daughter at once. Someone fetch a guard. This man stole my daughter."

One of the men who entered the room behind Adalric turned and strode from the room. Three others stood behind him and blocked the door so Hanun's servants couldn't enter.

"Can you prove she's your daughter?" Fen asked. "Do you have blood proof?"

Adalric turned to glare at Fen. "To think I offered

you space at my stables. You're no better than him." He gestured towards Hanun.

Before Hanun could speak, Fen stepped forward. "Only for your own advantage. How long would I have owned my dragon had I taken you up on your offer? Enough of that. Prove this is your daughter and you can take her."

Adalric turned to another of his men. "Ask my wife to send the birth blood. Have a wizard sent for. I'll prove before the guard this girl's my daughter." Adalric glared at them all, Edana included.

Silence filled the room as they waited, none of them interested in talking to each other. The silence was eventually broken by a scuffle outside the dining room and one of Hanun's servants called out, "Master, there's a letter from the competition arena." The man waved the letter above his head, still blocked from entering by Adalric's men.

"Read it out," Adalric ordered.

The servant looked towards Hanun. Fen answered for him. "Go ahead. Read it. We've nothing to hide."

"Yes, sir." The servant opened the letter. "After reviewing your dragon's races to date we have decided he is now of a standard to join the experienced level. This promotion will be in effect next Halfday competition."

"Huh! Now you'll see what real competition is. If I don't have a dragon in the experienced level races, Bastian does. There's no way you can win. We'll see who's laughing at the end of the races," Adalric gloated.

"River will still win," Edana said fiercely.

"It won't matter. You won't be there to see him win. You'll be locked in your room until your wedding day," Adalric warned.

A guard was ushered into the room. "Lords, you called for a guard?"

"This girl is my daughter. They've stolen her from me," Adalric pointed towards Edana.

"Do you now call this man father?" Fen asked Edana.

"No."

"My lord," the guard protested. "I can't take a girl from a home without proof."

"You'll have it. I've sent for blood proof and a wizard," Adalric said.

The guard turned towards Hanun and Fen. "Are you satisfied with this? Do you need your own wizard brought in to confirm the test?"

Fen shrugged. "We'll see what his wizard says. It'll depend on the honesty of the wizard. If he says her blood matches his daughter than we'll bring in our own wizard." Fen thought to River, *"I hope you told the truth about the blood being unrecognisable."*

"They will not compare. If the wizard says they do he lies."

"Honesty! My wizard is the most honest one around," Adalric bellowed.

"We'll soon see," Fen said.

As they waited, Hanun moved to Fen's side and muttered, "I hope you know what you're doing, boy."

Fen gave him a smile. "I do. I definitely do."

"I hope so. Especially when I know the truth of the matter."

Fen laughed. "Prepare to be amazed, Hanun."

"What are you two plotting?" Adalric demanded.

"I was wondering what we should spend out next lot of gold winnings on," Fen said.

"You have to win the race first. That won't happen," Adalric said.

Before anyone could reply, the servant arrived with the birth blood followed by the wizard. The men moved out of the doorway to let them into the room. Adalric explained the problem to the wizard.

"But that is your girl. Anyone can tell by looking at her. Surely everyone knows her look," the wizard protested.

"Never mind. Get this over with. I have more important things to do. I need to get ready for a betrothal ceremony," Adalric growled.

The wizard pulled a small silver bowl and a sharp instrument from within his robes. "Come here, mistress. I need some blood for the test."

Edana looked towards Fen. At his nod, she stepped forward and held out her hand. It was the one Fen had cut last night. There wasn't even a scar left behind to remind her of what she'd endured.

The wizard took her hand and beckoned one of Adalric's men forward to hold the bowl. A quick prick from the sharp instrument, a sudden indrawn breath from Edana and a few drops of blood fell into the bowl. The wizard let her hand go and Edana put her finger in her mouth to stop the blood from spilling.

"Are you all satisfied the blood came from the correct girl?" the wizard asked.

"Yes. Now get on with it." Adalric urged him on with an impatient gesture.

The wizard took the parchment with the birth blood on it. "Are you certain this is the blood you wish me to compare?"

"Of course I am. Do we have to go through all this nonsense?" Adalric demanded.

"Yes. All must be done correctly if we're to have a confirmed answer." The wizard turned to Fen and Hanun. "Are you happy with the proceedings so far?"

"Continue," Hanun said graciously.

The wizard turned to the man who held the bowl and started his spell. Several minutes later he stopped chanting and looked from Adalric to Fen.

"Well? Are you going to tell us the results?" Adalric demanded.

"Yes. Get it over and done with. Tell him the blood doesn't match," Fen said.

"Enough from you," Adalric snapped. He turned to the wizard. "Speak up. The guard is waiting to hear the results."

The wizard shook his head. "My lord," he faltered, unable to go on.

"What?" Adalric bellowed.

"The blood doesn't match." The words came out in a tumble and the wizard stepped back.

"Do the test again. Better yet. Bring me another wizard. Someone has cheated," Adalric yelled.

"We could take it to the courts. Have the court wizard do the test," the guard suggested. "There will still be a judge on duty. If there are other cases to be heard I am sure we can shuffle them around due to the urgency of this matter."

"Yes. I demand this be taken to the courts. I want a private audience. I want this dealt with now," Adalric ordered.

"Yes, my lord. Immediately," the guard agreed. "I'll meet you all there." He looked towards Edana. "If all involved parties are not there within the hour guards will be sent out to fetch them back."

Edana stepped forward. "My blood." She held her hand out to the wizard for the bowl. He gave it to her.

"That doesn't belong to her," Adalric argued.

"You can't have it if it doesn't match what you already own," the guard warned when Adalric started to step forward.

"What if she makes a run for it?" Adalric asked. "How will we find her?"

"I'll stand as her warranty. Would I risk my stables and dragon for someone I think will run?" Hanun asked.

"Will that be sufficient?" the guard asked Adalric.

"I gain his stable and dragon if the girl doesn't show up at the courts within the hour?" A look of calculation crossed Adalric's face.

"Yes," the guard confirmed.

"Then I'll expect you to escort me to the courts," Edana told the guard.

"It will be my pleasure." The guard gave a slight bow.

Fen stepped forward, with a linen napkin from the table, and took the bowl from Edana. He wiped it clean and tucked the napkin into his belt pouch. "Our insurance in case something should happen." He looked first at the guard and then at Adalric. He turned to Hanun. "You escort her to the courts. I'll keep watch on things here. With all this bad blood we wouldn't want to leave ourselves vulnerable." Fen stared at Hanun and hoped he'd understand and support him.

"Sensible. And of course I should be the one to go. I need to protect my investment." Hanun turned to Edana. "Come then, my dear. Let's sort this out."

The guard escorted Hanun and Edana to the courts.

Before he left to follow them, Adalric glared at Fen. "You've made yourself an enemy this day."

Fen smiled. "I made myself an enemy a long time before this."

"What's that supposed to mean?"

"The moment I officially owned my dragon you wanted him. I never planned to give him up. We've always been enemies."

Adalric growled before he stormed from the room.

As soon as he was confident everyone had left the house, Fen called the servants. He made certain they knew to lock the place up and let no one in. Once everything was secure, Fen walked to River's pen.

"Will she be fine?" Fen leaned against River for comfort.

"I will show you what happens. Through Edana's own eyes."

"You can do that?"

"If Edana will allow it." There was a moment of silence. *"She will allow it. She says she could do with the advice."*

Chapter Twenty-Seven

They joined Edana as she stood before the judge, the truthsayer at his side, while Adalric explained at the top of his voice what the problem was.

"Enough!" The judge bellowed loud enough to be heard over Adalric. "You girl, what is your name?"

"Answer him true," River warned. *"The truthsayer will test for honesty."*

"Edana Lenita Behira Yileen Renarlo con Crinitie," Edana answered.

"See. I told you this is my daughter," Adalric said.

"Enough." The judge glared at Adalric in annoyance. "Any more outbursts and you may leave my courts and I'll find in favour of the girl."

Adalric glared at him.

"Understood?" the judge asked.

"Yes, Your Honour," Adalric snapped.

"Now, girl. You give your name as this man's

daughter. Are you not here to prove you aren't his daughter? You'd best not be wasting my time."

"No, Your Honour. This man claims me as his daughter and has brought the birth blood to prove it. His wizard tested me and it came up negative. The blood says I'm not his daughter," Edana said, prompted by River and Fen.

"How can this be possible?" the judge asked.

Edana shrugged. She knew there was no verbal answer she could give without a lie being detected.

The judge turned to Adalric. "What happened to your daughter? Why does this one not match?"

"This is my daughter. The wizard must have cheated. There's no other answer. I want the test done again," Adalric demanded.

The judge nodded and a wizard stepped forward. The same procedure as before was done again. The wizard looked between all the parties before he stepped close to the judge. They whispered between themselves before the judge turned to glare at Adalric.

"Did you or any of your people cause the death of your birth child?" the judge demanded.

"No!"

"Send for his wife," the judge told one of his men. With a nod the man left.

"What's the meaning of this? My daughter's here before you." Adalric pointed towards Edana.

The judge looked around the room solemnly. "I don't know who this girl is, but her blood shows she's not your daughter. I can only think foul play was involved."

There was a bellow from Adalric and he threw himself at Hanun. Guards pulled him away and held him as he strained to attack his brother.

"This is something he's cooked up. Ask him what he knows," Adalric snarled, still trying to reach Hanun.

"You'll be fined for this outburst in my court," the judge said to Adalric. He turned towards Hanun. "What do you know about this?"

"I always thought her my niece. I was as amazed as you the first time I saw that test come up negative," Hanun said.

"My blood shows me not to be his daughter? Does this mean I can freely leave his house?" Edana asked.

"No!" Adalric shouted.

"The fine will be increased." The judge shot a glare at Adalric before he turned to Edana. "The birth blood shows he has no claim on you. Have you anywhere to go?"

"Yes, thank you," Edana said.

The judge nodded. "We cannot have a young woman who's been raised in the upper classes fend for herself. You'd have no skills with which to earn your living."

"She's my daughter," Adalric argued.

The courtroom doors opened and guards escorted Edana's mother, Behira, inside. She looked as perfectly made up as ever and her face showed no emotion.

"State your name please," the judge said when Behira reached the front of the courtroom.

"Behira Carlea Girra Crinitie con Eladorro."

"And who is this young woman here?" The judge pointed to Edana.

"My daughter, Edana Lenita Behira Yileen Renarlo con Crinitie."

"The blood test shows otherwise. According to the blood test this is not the child you gave birth to. Have you or any of your people or have you asked anyone to cause the death of the child you gave birth to, dispose of the child you gave birth to or in any way have you rid yourself of the child you gave birth to either deliberately or accidentally?"

The first sign of emotion appeared on Behira's face. It was shock. "No."

The judge stared at them thoughtfully. "This

young woman is now her own person. She will have to choose a new family name. There is no offspring to be registered to Behira and Adalric. The child will be listed dead. This is my final ruling."

Adalric began to shout and Behira looked dazed for a moment before she started to wail. The judge had them escorted from the courtroom before he turned to Edana.

"You may keep your given names if you wish, but you will need to choose a new family name."

"I don't know what to choose," Edana said softly.

"We need a name to register you. You'll be listed as an orphan," the judge explained.

"I'd be honoured if you'd take my name, Edana," Hanun said.

"Well, I guess," Edana said uncertainly.

"It is a good choice. If there is any doubt in your father's mind he will wash his hands of you for that choice alone," River told Edana.

"Yes. Carson it will be," Edana said more firmly.

"Do you wish to be listed as Hanun's adopted daughter?" the judge asked.

Edana shook her head. "No. I wish to be my own person."

"Orphan it is then," the judge said.

A clerk entered the information into the record books and made a copy for Edana.

Once outside the courtrooms, Hanun hugged her. "I don't know what happened in there, but welcome to my home."

"Thank you. We should head back to Fen and River."

"A celebration tonight," Hanun said heartily.

Edana laughed. "It looks that way. Especially with River going to the next level of races."

"I nearly forgot about that in all the excitement," Hanun said. "Well, I've a party to plan. Better get moving."

Fen was relieved to see everything turn out well. He was disorientated when River broke the link with Edana. His surroundings were hazy and he could barely focus on anything in the pen.

Mouse burst into the pen. The door hit the wall and flew back towards him. He jumped out of the way in time. "The eggs are hatching."

"Eggs?" Fen tried to gather his scattered thoughts.

"Pearl's eggs. River and Pearl's eggs. One of them has cracks in it. I checked on them like you told me to do every four hours. It's got cracks," Mouse said.

Fen staggered to his feet, River nudged him in the

back when he would have stumbled. "Do you want to come River?"

"I will wait."

"Come on," Mouse said impatiently.

Chapter Twenty-Eight

With each step he took, Fen started to feel better. By the time they reached the room where the eggs were kept, he felt like himself. He stood in front of the four eggs gathered around a heat stone. One of them had a crack in it. A scratching sound came from inside and it rocked slightly.

Mouse pointed at the egg. "See. It's hatching."

Fen moved closer and hovered over the egg as he watched it rock harder. The crack widened. Fen had to stop himself from helping.

"I just heard," Edana said breathlessly as she ran into the room. "I haven't missed it, have I?"

Fen glanced over at her. "Congratulations on your new identity."

Edana grinned. "Yes, but I nearly missed this." She pointed to the egg that rocked again. "I can't wait till it hatches. River's first baby."

"Don't go getting mushy," Fen said. "We're selling them, remember?"

"Surely not the first one."

Fen shrugged. "I don't know. We have no dragons to breed them with. We only have the parents."

"I'm getting too old for this." Hanun came into the room, also out of breath.

Edana grinned at him. "Isn't it exciting? Why don't Pearl and River want to be here to greet their new baby?"

"They need to see humans. They must understand you will be the ones they answer to," River thought to both of them.

"Oh, I never thought of that. They aren't really their parents' children. They belong to those who'll sell them," Edana said.

"They're dragons, not humans. You talk as if they were slaves," Hanun said.

"Hush Edana. It is our punishment for the sins of our fathers. Those that attacked humans are cursed to forever serve them."

"That's so unfair," Edana wailed.

"Edana," Fen warned.

"What?"

"Stop talking to yourself," Fen glanced over at Hanun.

"Sorry. Oh, look." Edana pointed at the egg. "It's going to split right open."

Edana had no sooner finished speaking than a large piece of the egg cracked with a grating pop and fell to the surface the eggs rested on. A head pushed up through the hole and was soon followed by shoulders. The dragon let out a squawk, as it looked around at the people who stared speechless at it.

"It's… it's," Edana couldn't finish.

Mouse helped her with an explosive, "Red."

The egg tipped over and the dragon tumbled out and moved awkwardly to the edge.

"Oh, you're so adorable," Edana crooned as she swept the dragon into her arms. She yelped, nearly dropping the dragon. "It bit me!"

Fen laughed as Edana put the dragon near the eggshell. "Maybe it's hungry."

"I'll get food." Mouse scurried away.

"She. Her mother calls her Carmine," River told Edana and Fen.

"How appropriate," Edana said.

"What?" Hanun asked.

"Oh." Edana looked over at Fen who grinned at her discomfit. "We should call her Carmine. Don't you think that's appropriate?"

"Excellent name," Hanun agreed.

"Nice save," Fen whispered as he moved near Edana before he leaned in for a closer look at Carmine. "Has anyone ever heard of a dragon being born coloured?" He looked between Edana and Hanun. Both shook their heads.

"Not that I'd really know. Most of my knowledge comes from books," Hanun said.

"My father's stables had thousands of babies born there during my life and not one of them was coloured at birth. I should know with the amount of time I spent in the stables. I could tell you about every lineage of every dragon he ever had and the colours of the offspring and the average time it took them to change," Edana said.

"I don't think we should let this get about. Who knows what it could mean," Fen said.

Hanun nodded thoughtfully. "We don't want people prying into our business."

"Master." A servant rapped on the door.

Fen shook his head and quickly made sure his body blocked all view of the dragon before Hanun opened the door and stepped out.

"Master. There's a crazy woman outside looking for Mistress Edana," the servant said.

Fen looked over at Edana who shrugged. "I'll come with you. As soon as Mouse returns."

Edana nodded. They both slipped out of the room.

"You heard?" Hanun asked.

Edana nodded. "I can't imagine who it'd be."

"Probably your mother," Hanun said.

"My mother is as far as one can get from a crazy woman," Edana protested.

"The typical stone statue," Fen said in agreement.

"I've got the food." Mouse joined them. "What you all doing?" He looked at each of them.

"I'm leaving you in charge, Mouse. The only ones allowed to enter are Hanun, Edana or myself. Is that understood?" Fen asked.

Mouse stood taller. "Not even a lizard'll get past me."

Fen nodded and followed Hanun as he made his way to the front door. Edana at his side.

Fen glanced towards her. "Whoever it is can't take you from here. We made sure of that today."

"I know. And thank you."

"It was as much your doing as mine. Besides, now we're even." Fen grinned fleetingly.

Chapter Twenty-Nine

Hanun reached the front door first. "Madame Crinitie con Eladorro."

"Madame. Not for much longer," Behira spat.

Edana ran forward. "Mother."

"Don't call me that. Don't ever call me that again. How could you?" Behira demanded.

"How could I what?"

"You've given Adalric grounds for divorce. You're no longer his heir. That means I didn't provide him with an heir during the first five years of our marriage. He can divorce me. I'll have nothing. The pittance the law says he is to provide me with is a laugh," Behira yelled.

"He's divorcing you?" Edana took a step back from Behira.

"Of course he is. What did you expect? That he'd still call you heir after you threw our parenting in our face. Since you no longer want us as your parents, you can no longer inherit the stables." Behira laughed bitterly. "How naïve are you?"

Edana shook her head. "I didn't think he'd let me inherit, but–"

"There are no buts. If he hasn't an heir then he must get one. I'm too old. He needs a younger bride," Behira said. "Oh, what's to become of me? I'm in disgrace. Not even my family want me back."

"Surely–" Edana began.

"Nothing. I'll have nothing. Do you know how many years I had to put up with him? I spent my life as little more than his slave, expecting to be kept like a queen till my death. And now I find you aren't his heir. Why? Why did you tell him? You could have inherited the stables."

"No, I couldn't. I wasn't the son he wanted. A son of mine would have inherited the stables. I wasn't staying there to be ruled by a husband so my son could have the stables."

"You're mad!" Behira shouted.

Edana shook her head. "No. I'm just not you. I can't be someone I'm not. I have to live my life by my terms."

"As a pauper? You have nothing now," Behira yelled.

"She has friends. True friends who'll be there for her no matter what she has to go through." Fen stepped forward to stand by Edana's side. "That's worth more than gold."

"Another fool. What would you know about having no money?" Behira demanded.

Fen laughed bitterly. "More than you could imagine, Madame. And with good friends I was able to move far from poverty."

"She's not without wealth," Hanun said. "She has a choice of four dragons that are now hatching. She won't be dependant on anyone. She can make her own way in the world. On her own terms."

"Hanun, you don't have to," Edana protested.

Hanun smiled. "I won't have my niece a pauper."

Behira laughed crazily. "But she's not your niece. You were there. Didn't you understand?"

Hanun shrugged. "Blood doesn't matter. I can see with my own two eyes she's my niece. What does a stupid test matter to me?"

"Oh everything. Simply everything." Behira turned to glare at Edana. "I never knew you hated me this much. I would've smothered you at birth and had another child if I had known how you'd turn out."

Edana started to take another step back from the anger directed at her. Fen dropped an arm around her shoulders and moved closer. She took a deep breath. "I never hated you. How can you hate a person you don't know? I knew my father better than I knew you. All you were was the woman who brought me out to show off at suitable times and yelled at me for being an inconvenience at others. I learned to stay out of your way. So I never knew you. I feel sorry for you, but I don't hate you."

"I don't need your sympathy. And don't come looking to me for any when you find here is no better than what you had." With a last wild look, Behira spun around and stormed out of the house.

Fen patted Edana's shoulder his hand rested on. "You won't need to go looking for sympathy from that woman, Eddie. We'll look out for you."

"What a dreadful name," Hanun exclaimed. "Surely you don't call her Eddie?"

Edana laughed at the shocked expression on Hanun's face. "I'm afraid he does."

They returned to the eggs to find Mouse pacing back and forth. "What took you so long?" Mouse demanded as soon as they entered.

Fen glanced at the dragon. Seeing she was fine, he asked, "What's wrong?"

Mouse pointed towards Carmine. "She's evil. She

spat her food at me. She knocked on the other eggs. She even tried to push one of the eggs onto the floor."

"Oh dear," Edana said. "What are we going to do with her?"

"Bring her," River told Fen and Edana.

"What have we got to wrap her in?" Fen asked Mouse.

"A hessian bag with two rocks in it?" Mouse asked hopefully.

"Just the bag," Fen said.

Mouse glared at Carmine. "I hope you're not expecting me to put her in the bag. She nearly drew blood before."

Fen suppressed a grin. "I'll do it."

As soon as Mouse brought the hessian bag, Fen tried to slip it over Carmine. She hissed and scratched and made every effort to attack him. After a great deal of struggling and some help from Edana, Fen managed to get Carmine in the bag.

"I can't imagine what the problem is," Hanun said. "I've never heard of tame dragons carrying on like this. Do you think it has something to do with the fact their father's a wild grey?"

"I don't know what the problem is," Fen said. "I guess we'll have to wait and see what happens when the other three hatch."

"What will we do if they're all wild?" Edana asked.

Fen grinned at her. "Looks like you won't be a wealthy woman after all."

Edana hit Fen on the arm. "Grow up."

"Children. Careful of that dragon," Hanun warned.

"I'll take her to River. See if he can sort her out," Fen said.

"I'll stay here with Mouse. I'll help him keep an eye on these other eggs. They usually all hatch within twenty-four hours of each other," Hanun said.

"I'll go with Fen." Edana followed him to the door. "We shouldn't be too long. I want to see them hatch too."

As soon as Edana and Fen had left Carmine with River, they returned to wait for the eggs to hatch. Hanun had dinner delivered and it wasn't until the early hours of the next morning the last three eggs hatched. They were all born grey.

"I wonder why Carmine was different," Edana said.

"I don't know, but I think we should wait to have the officials register the births," Fen said.

"They only give us two days to notify them," Hanun warned.

"I know. We'll wait the full two days. Then we can say Carmine changed colour not long before they arrived. That's possible," Fen said.

Hanun nodded slowly. "That might be best. Although I don't know how they're going to get close enough to her to take blood for the registration. It'll have to be done. It's the law. I just don't know how they'll manage it."

Fen grinned. "At least it'll be interesting to see them try."

Hanun slowly shook his head. "I worry over the things that amuse you, boy."

Carmine was still violent two days later when it was time to register her and her siblings. The other three dragons had changed colour and there was a blue female called Brook, a green male called Forest and a female the same colour as her mother called Lace. River had told them the names given them by their mother. Hanun didn't mind what the dragons were called and Fen and Edana didn't tell him where the names came from.

When it was time for the officials to take blood from Carmine, River held her down with one paw while the officials hovered nervously at the door of his pen.

"This isn't the way it's normally done," the first official, Algis, said.

"The dragon should be with its egg mates. That's

the way it's always done," Norwell, the second official, said.

Fen looked over at River and he let his daughter go. The moment the pressure was off, she hissed and snapped and threw herself at the officials. Seconds before she reached them, as they tried to quickly exit the pen, River grabbed her and held her down again.

"Can we get this over and done with? I'm sure River would like to stop holding her at some stage today," Fen said.

"She's wild. You'll have to release her," Algis said.

"She's the offspring of a wild dragon," Fen said. "What did you expect?"

"Well," Norwell looked over at Algis as if he might have the answer.

"I've read every ruling regarding hatchlings and there's nothing that says dragons born in captivity must be returned to the wild if they act like a wild dragon," Fen said.

"Impossible. There must be something," Algis said. Norwell shook his head. "Not that I can think of."

"There must be," Algis said.

"There's nothing," Hanun said. "Now take her blood so she can be registered."

"We'll be looking into this further," Algis warned.

"That's fine," Hanun said. "You'll find nothing.

My lawyers have also scoured the rulebooks and laws regarding this issue and found not one ruling about it. Now take her blood and be done with it."

Algis took a sharp instrument and with a quick jab in a thin skinned area waited for a few drops of blood to well up. As soon as enough appeared, Algis touched a piece of parchment to the blood and then moved away hurriedly.

"Name?" Algis readied his quill and ink.

"Carmine," Hanun said.

"Out of," Algis asked.

"River and Pearl of Carson Dragon Stables," Hanun said.

"Registered to." Algis kept his eyes on the parchment.

"Carson Dragon Stables," Hanun answered.

"Will the owners read and sign the details." Algis handed the parchment over to Hanun.

As they had done with the other three dragons, Hanun and Fen read the information and signed it. The parchment went into the leather case that would be used to transport it to the records building where it would be bound into a leather book of all the dragons born that month as well as cross-referenced in several other books.

"Good day to you," Algis said frostily. Norwell nodded.

The moment they were all out of the pen, River licked his daughter's blood spot to heal it and let her go.

"What are we going to do with her?" Hanun asked wearily.

"I don't know." Fen sighed heavily. "She's been different from the start. Who knows what to expect from her?"

"We might have to end up setting her free. We can't force her to stay here if her whole life will be one of imprisonment," Edana said.

"We're going to have to get her a separate pen from River. It makes it too difficult when we need to train him," Hanun said.

"We'll put a door between the pen next to River's and then he can send her into her own room when we need to come in," Fen said.

"How do you expect him to be able to do that?" Hanun asked.

"I can do it," River told Fen and Edana.

"He'll manage," Fen said with a smile.

Chapter Thirty

The next Halfday, the first person Fen ran into after he'd settled River at the competition grounds was Adalric. He stood inside the owners' area and bragged to one of his friends about the speed of his dragon, Twilight. He stopped in mid sentence when he saw Fen.

"You have a nerve showing up here," Adalric said.

At that same moment, Hanun and Edana joined Fen and Adalric's eyes narrowed as he glared at them.

"All of you have a nerve," Adalric growled.

"I don't see why we shouldn't show up," Fen said.

"You steal my daughter, you destroy my line and then you show up here where you knew I'd be," Adalric argued.

Fen smiled mildly. "You destroyed your own line. And I showed up here because River plans to take another gold."

"Gold. Not a chance. He's racing against my Twilight. She's never been beaten. And not only that, one of the out of town dragons, Black Star, is in the same race."

"What do you think, River?" Fen sent his thoughts towards where he knew River was stabled.

"I have seen them both. They do not care where they come in the race. There is no reason for them to win. They race because it is expected of them. I will take gold for you, Fen," River assured him.

"River will take gold," Fen said firmly.

"A wager. We must have a wager," one of Adalric's friends said.

"Something worth wagering over," another said.

Bastian came to stand with them. "A wager. How interesting."

Adalric gave a curt nod in greeting. "Bastian."

"Adalric." Bastian gave the same curt nod back.

"Are we to have a wager? How about the one who is first is paid by the ones who come after him," one of the bystanders suggested.

"No. Money takes the fun out of it." Bastian shook his head. "I won't be in any wager that's so uninteresting."

"Afraid you'll lose?" Adalric asked.

"Certainly not. Firefly was moved into Twilight's

race. My usual dragon for the race is mating," Bastian said.

"Ah, Firefly, she's only lost once, hasn't she?" Hanun glanced towards Adalric.

"To one of my dragons I believe," Adalric said smugly.

"Not to Twilight though," Bastian quickly replied.

"Only because she's never raced against her," Adalric said.

"It doesn't matter, gentlemen," Hanun interrupted. "Our River will take the gold so you're wasting your time. Lay a wager with us if you will, but be prepared to pay at the end."

"Pay! It'll be you doing the paying," Adalric hissed.

"What sort of wager?" Bastian asked.

Hanun hummed as he tapped his lip thoughtfully. "What about the two who lose out of us three must give the winner a recently hatched female dragon?"

"Unheard of," exclaimed one of the bystanders.

"Completely mad," another cried out.

"Unless you're both worried you'll lose." Hanun looked first at Adalric and then at Bastian.

Edana elbowed Fen, glaring at him when he turned to look at her. "Do something," she hissed.

"I guess you're right, Hanun. They have no faith in their dragons at all," Fen said.

"That wasn't what I meant." Edana kicked Fen's shin to make him stop.

"Agreed," Adalric held out his hand to Fen. He shook it and then turned to Bastian.

"Yes. Agreed." Bastian shook first Adalric's hand and then Fen's.

"Someone fetch a bookmaker. We need to make this official. I don't want anyone trying to get out of paying me my two young female dragons," Adalric said.

"No. I certainly don't want you trying to weasel out when it's my Firefly who wins," Bastian said.

A bookmaker soon arrived and he wrote down the wager in his book with relish. Within minutes he was taking bets with people over who'd be collecting the wager.

"If you'll excuse me," Fen said. "I'm going to find a good spot to view the race from." He started to move away.

"Make sure you don't go too far. I wouldn't want to have to go looking for you to arrange delivery of my new dragon," Adalric said.

Fen paused and turned to face Adalric across the crowd. "I'm partial to grey myself. I've done well with mine. So make it a female that hasn't come into her colour yet." He turned and strode back through the crowd before Adalric had a chance to reply.

"Are you mad?" Edana demanded in an angry whisper when Fen had found a place to view the arena from.

Fen grinned. "Probably."

"And you're just as bad," Edana turned on Hanun.

"Nothing ventured, nothing gained," Hanun said.

"You only have four baby dragons and you're wagering one of them away," Edana said.

"Three," Hanun said. "Did you forget we gave one to you?"

"Two after today. And how many will be left by the end of the week? Or the end of the month? You can't go throwing them away like that." Edana glared at them both, hands on her hips.

"I've risked everything before and come out on top," Fen reminded Edana.

"That was different," Edana said.

Fen stared silently at Edana and willed her to understand. "Sometimes life's a gamble. We can't pass up this chance, Eddie. With two more female dragons we can increase our breeding stock dramatically. As it is we can't keep any of our dragons for breeding because they're all related. Do you think any of this lot are likely to sell us a dragon? Adalric will make certain they don't."

Edana sighed. "I hope River knows what's at stake."

"I do. I will win. No more fretting," River told them both.

"I hope so," Edana muttered.

"Enough quarrelling," Hanun said. "The race is starting."

Fen and Edana moved forward to stand with Hanun, their eyes glued to the door where the dragons would enter the arena. As the dragons entered, the announcer called out each of their names and stable.

Fen took that time to remind River of the course. Then the race began and River was fourth in the pack. The competition was tougher than usual. The dragons he competed against were accustomed to the longer and more difficult course. Fen sent picture after picture to show River where the other dragons were in comparison to him and he was able to weave amongst them as they glided through the spires. He gained third place and was close to second when they reached the last spire before the open straight to the first checkpoint. The dragons in the lead spread out. A dragon barrelled in from behind and shouldered

River into the last spire. He hit with a thud and the officials ordered the dragon from the arena.

Chapter Thirty-One

"Pull up," Fen thought frantically to River as the ground came closer. *"Pull up and away."* Fen felt Edana's hand reach out and clasp his. They both watched as River struggled to regain height.

"Foul!" Hanun bellowed beside them. "I bet it's Adalric behind it. He couldn't win a fair race even if he tried."

"He's gaining height," Edana whispered. "Come on, River. You can do it."

Fen held Edana's hand tightly as he watched the other dragons come back from the checkpoint and pass the still floundering River.

"Get him far away from the spires," Edana whispered. "There'll be at least one other willing to try. It's a classic Adalric/Bastian technique."

"Scum," Hanun called out.

"Come on, River," Fen pleaded.

River worked his wings hard and pulled upwards. One wing didn't appear to work as hard as the other and he seemed to almost fly on an angle.

"Don't let them beat us, River. You promised me gold. Take it from them," Fen urged.

Fen held his breath as River surged ahead to the checkpoint and turned back to the spires. With no other dragons in his way he was able to take the spires close. He pulled his wings tight against his body so he nearly brushed against them. As he gained on the second checkpoint he came closer to the rest of the dragons. Past the checkpoint he overtook several.

"That's it," Fen urged as he sent picture after picture to show where all the other dragons were located compared to River.

"He's doing it." Edana bounced on the spot, still clasping Fen's hand tightly.

River reached fourth place as they came close to the last spire before the third checkpoint. Fen saw the dragons spread out again and one of the dragons come in from behind.

"Not again," Edana shrieked.

"Get away from him, River," Hanun bellowed as he leaned forward and clenched his fists.

"Drop down, to the right," Fen ordered River. The dragon tried to swerve and take him again. They

were past the spires and headed for the checkpoint. *"Watch him on the way back,"* Fen warned River.

River tailed Twilight, staying as close to her as possible.

"What are you doing?" Fen demanded of River.

River ignored him and flew on as they headed for the spires again. Fen sent him images of where the other dragons were. He was Twilight's shadow. She tried to move away as they reached the first spire. The other dragon came in fast. River dropped below Twilight at the last second. The dragon barrelled into Twilight instead and she hit the spire and plummeted to the ground.

The rest of the dragons flew on and the official ordered the other dragon out of the arena.

"Yes!" Hanun's fist punched the sky.

River was now in third place. Twilight limped off the field, her trainer by her side. Black Star was in the lead with Firefly close behind him. River was close on their tails, but he quickly gained on them. Firefly took the lead by a head. River was level with Black Star. They came close to the last spire before the last checkpoint.

"Keep watch," Fen warned River.

The dragons stayed in close formation. Then they were on the last straight. Edana's fingernails dug into

Fen's hand. He sent picture after picture. All three dragons were neck and neck, coming in for the last checkpoint. The crowd fell completely silent as if they all held their breath. Hanun clung to the rail between the owner's area and the arena and leaned forward as if he could help River go faster.

"Go River," Edana whispered.

River put on a last burst of speed and his large wings pushed him through the air. He tucked them close to his body as he shot through the small gap between the two lead dragons. The crowd roared in excitement as the three dragons flew past the final checkpoint, River barely in the lead.

"He did it," Edana squealed as she jumped up and down. She threw her arms around Fen and hugged him tight. She then turned to Hanun and threw her arms around him.

Fen smiled. He was too exhausted to do anything else. "*You did it,*" he thought to River.

"*I told you I would,*" River answered.

"*So you did,*" Fen told him. "*Are you well? No problems from that hit?*"

"*Some tenderness. I will be fine.*"

"We have to see River. He deserves pampering for a year." Edana still grinned.

"For life," Hanun said. "I can't wait to see Adalric's face." Hanun's hands rubbed together.

But Adalric was gone. No one knew where he was.

"Coward," Hanun exclaimed when they reached home to find Adalric had sent over a two-month-old grey female dragon with a servant. "Should have known he couldn't bring himself to deliver it. A true gentleman always pays his wagers in person."

Not long after they arrived a servant informed them Bastian waited to see them. Hanun had him shown in. With him was a servant carrying a grey dragon.

After greetings were out of the way, Bastian said, "I hope you were serious when you said you were partial to grey."

Fen laughed. "Definitely."

"Rather unconventional whelp, isn't he?" Hanun said fondly.

"Hey, grey's been good to me," Fen protested.

"I'll warn you this one is nearly three-months-old." Bastian smiled. "It was too good an opportunity to pass up."

Fen laughed. "Pay a debt and rid yourself of a nuisance all at once."

Bastian chuckled. "You've obviously worked out how to protect your dragon from being stolen. Most of us have a hard time keeping our losses to less than three a year. A permanent grey is too much of a draw card."

Fen shrugged. "We keep what's ours."

"You'll have to give me pointers some time. And if you're interested, I have a few female dragons ready to mate at the moment. You might like to pair them with your River," Bastian suggested.

Once again Fen shrugged. "Mating would have to occur here. The eggs would be raised here and I'd expect first choice. It would all be done by written agreement."

"That's unusual. Normally the eggs are raised in the stable of the female dragon," Bastian said.

"That's our terms. Take them or leave them. You've already pointed out your security isn't as good as ours."

Bastian stared at Fen thoughtfully. "I suppose I did." He nodded. "I'll send my lawyers around with the paperwork Firstday."

"I look forward to doing business with you," Fen said.

They continued with small talk until Bastian left.

As soon as he'd gone, Edana turned to Fen. "We've made it. We've actually made it." She clutched his hands.

Hanun laughed. "You were the best thing to ever happen in this household, boy. You and that dragon of yours."

Fen smiled. He squeezed Edana's hands in acknowledgement of her comment. "River was the best thing that happened to all of us."

Chapter Thirty-Two

Fen looked at the metal cage on the back of the wagon. He felt a wave of reassurance wash over him and glanced towards River who waited at the rear of the wagon. Edana slipped her hand in his and he looked down at her.

"I know you don't want to let her go-" Edana began.

"She's still too young. What if she gets hurt? Who'll look after her?" Fen's eyes were drawn to Carmine where she crouched in the cage. She hissed.

"It's for the best. She doesn't like people, she hates horses and barely tolerates her parents. She's more ferocious than a wild dragon. Even River said it's best to let her go."

"I know, but she's still so little." Fen frowned as he watched Carmine swipe at the side of the cage.

"She's six-months-old. Not that little. And I don't

think she's going to let anything come close enough to hurt her." Edana squeezed Fen's hand in reassurance.

Fen glanced around. They were at the edge of a heavily treed area. Ahead of them were jagged mountains, where very few ventured. It was the perfect place to release a dragon that didn't want company of any description. He sighed heavily and ran his free hand through his hair. Fen released Edana's hand and moved towards the horse. As soon as she was unhitched, he led her towards the trees. Edana walked beside him. Once they were under the shelter of the trees, River opened the cage and stepped back.

Carmine hissed at her father as she moved past him. He didn't react to her anger. Instead his eyes followed her as she took to the sky and flew towards the mountains.

"She'll be happier now," Edana said softly.

Fen nodded. "I know. I just wish we could've figured out why she's like that."

"People don't usually breed from tame greys. Maybe this has something to do with it."

"The others are perfect. And look to have their father's speed." Fen grinned. "Be nice to take a few more first places."

"That'll really impress my father."

"And his new wife." Fen laughed as Edana rolled her eyes.

"I can't believe he married Bastian's daughter. She's not much older than me. And he's so old."

"It makes sense. The two most important families. The child they have will nearly own this town."

"Only if they have a boy," Edana reminded him.

"I've got a feeling your father won't stick with having one child this time."

"Probably not. But I can't believe how young his wife is."

Fen led the horse back to the wagon. "At least you won't be expected to call her Ma."

Edana shook her head. "I wouldn't have even if he still saw me as his daughter."

"They're not worth worrying about." Fen held out his hand to help Edana onto the seat of the wagon.

"I know. It's just strange being treated like I'm invisible when we're at the same function as my father."

"You're better off without him."

"He isn't a bad person. It's the way he was raised."

"Just 'cause you're raised some way, doesn't mean you have to live that way the rest of your life."

"No." Edana smiled. "I'm glad you came into my father's stable that night."

Fen looked into her eyes, before he slowly nodded. "Me too." He turned to the horse and shook the reins. "We better get back before Mouse eats all that feast Hanun's organising to celebrate River's fiftieth win."

Edana burst into laughter. "I'm sure Hanun has enough to feed an army. He's so proud of River." Edana glanced upwards to where River flew above them. "Not that I blame him."

"I wonder what Hanun will do to celebrate a hundred wins."

"Don't pressure River," Edana said.

"Pressure him! He loves to win. Don't you?" Fen glanced upwards.

"Of course I do. Hanun can look forward to his party to celebrate one hundred wins. I will keep flying in several races each Halfday," River thought to them.

"See, he loves to win," Fen said.

Edana shook her head. "I don't want him to wear himself out."

"He won't. No point entering a race if he's too exhausted to win. That'd defeat the purpose."

"Defeat the–" Edana stopped abruptly. "My father's prize dragons. That's the races you enter."

"You're a bit slow on it, Ed. We thought you'd have figured it out before now." Fen grinned at her.

"Why?"

"A few reasons. But the main one is he hurt you and locked you up. Taking you from him didn't bother him enough. He's planning on replacing you. So we found something that would hurt. He hates to lose. And he's lost a lot in the past six months."

Edana touched Fen lightly on the forearm. She blinked rapidly and cleared her throat. "You didn't need to do that for me."

"It wasn't just for you. It was for River and me too. He tried to kill River because he never changed colour. And then when everyone thought River was a wild dragon, he tried to steal him from me. We owed him for that too."

"He's going to hate you for life."

Fen grinned. "Good. That'd mean we really bothered him."

They fell into contented silence as the town came into view. River flew above, watching over them and the wagon bounced along the rarely used track as they drove home.

Free Ebook

Subscribe to Avril's newsletter to receive a free ebook. This ebook is exclusive to those on her mailing list. To find out more about this offer visit: http://www.avrilsabine.com/free-ebook/

*

We value your privacy and will not sell, rent, exchange or loan your email address to third parties. Your information is confidential and you are under no obligation to remain on the mailing list and can unsubscribe at any time.

Acknowledgements

Thank you to all those who helped, particularly Jo-ann, Talitha and especially my kids who don't mind in the least pointing out any story problems.

To The Reader

If you enjoyed this book, why not consider leaving a review to help other readers discover it too? Reader engagement is one of the few ways that lets an author know readers want more books in a particular series or genre. So leave a review and tell friends, not only about this book but also about other ones you've enjoyed, so you can continue to enjoy books by your favourite authors for years to come.

Dreams are meant to be lived,

Avril.

About The Author

Avril is an Australian author who lives with her family on acreage in South East Queensland. She writes mostly young adult speculative fiction, but has been known to dabble in other genres. You can find more information about her at her website www.avrilsabine.com where you can also subscribe to her newsletter to be kept informed about new releases, current projects, blog posts and exclusive news.

Titles By Avril Sabine

Stories about strong characters and characters who discover their strengths.

SERIES

Assassins Of The Dead- Young Adult Fantasy/ Paranormal

Book 1: Dark Blade

Book 2: Dragon Touched

Book 3: Society Against Vampires

Book 4: King's Request

Dragon Blood- Young Adult Urban Fantasy (with elements of romance)

(5 book series)

Book 1: Pliethin

Book 2: Wyvern

Book 3: Surety

Book 4: Knight

Book 5: Mage

Dragon Mage- Young Adult Urban Fantasy (with elements of romance)

(Series two of Dragon Blood series)

Book 1: Promise

Dragon Blood Chronicles- Young Adult Urban Fantasy (with elements of romance)

(Companion stand alone series to Dragon Blood)

Book 1: Oath

Book 2: Betrayed

Guardians Of The Round Table- Young Adult Fantasy LitRPG

(Co-written with Storm and Rhys Petersen)

Book 1: Dexterity Fail

Book 2: Goblin Boots

Book 3: Singed Feathers

Book 4: Frog Mage

Book 5: Crystal Mine

Book 6: Cursed Harp

Rosie's Rangers- Young Adult Western Steampunk

(6 book series)

Book 1: Justice

Book 2: Vengeance

Book 3: Treachery

Book 4: Accused

Book 5: Wanted

Book 6: Corruption

Mark Of Kings- Children's Fantasy

(Upper middle grade/preteen)

(4 book series)

Book 1: The Arena

Book 2: The Island

Book 3: The Assassin

Book 4: The King

STAND ALONE SERIES

*Demon Hunters- Young Adult Urban Fantasy/
Horror (with elements of romance)*

Book 1: Blood Sacrifice

Book 2: Retribution

Book 3: Tainted

Book 4: Premonition

Book 5: Cursed

Book 6: Feud

Book 7: Extrication

Plea Of The Damned- Young Adult Urban Fantasy/Paranormal

(6 book series)

Book 1: Forgive Me Lucy

Book 2: Forgive Me Aiden

Book 3: Forgive Me Jena

Book 4: Forgive Me Kobe

Book 5: Forgive Me Marti

Book 6: Forgive Me Dawson

Realms Of The Fae- Young Adult Urban Fantasy (with elements of romance)

The Sword (short story in Like A Girl Anthology)

Heart Of Stone

Book 1: A Debt Owed

Book 2: Marked By The Hunt

Book 3: The Magic Collector

Book 4: An Unexpected Betrayal

Book 5: Imprisoned By Iron

Fairytales Retold (Short Stories)

Snow-White And Rose-Red

The Twelve Brothers

The Light Princess

Beauty And The Beast

Sleeping Beauty

Aschenputtel

The Golden Bird

The Frog Prince

The Death Of Koshchei The Deathless

Myths And Legends Retold (Short Stories)

Ion, Son Of Apollo

Sir Gawain And The Maid With The Narrow Sleeves

Princess Ilse, The Giant's Daughter

YOUNG ADULT NOVELS

Young Adult Fantasy (with elements of romance)

Elf Sight

Earth Bound

Young Adult Urban Fantasy

Stone Warrior (with elements of romance)

The Jungle Inside

Young Adult Contemporary (with elements of romance)

Through Your Eyes

The Ugly Stepsister

Perfect Little Princess

Young Adult Contemporary/Paranormal

Whispers In The Dark (with elements of romance and same sex relationships)

Over Too Soon (with elements of romance)

Young Adult Sci-Fi

Experiment X-One-Six (Urban Sci-Fi/Superheroes)

An Endless Dawn (Post Apocalyptic Sci-Fi)

CHILDREN'S BOOKS

Dragon Lord (Preteen/early teens) (Fantasy)

The Irish Wizard (Upper middle grade) (Urban Fantasy)

SHORT STORIES

Urban Fantasy

Eternally Late

Dealings With Joe

Glimpses (short story in That Moment When Anthology)

Contemporary

The Brat Next Door

Fantasy LitRPG

(Set in the same world as Guardians Of The Round Table Series)

Tales Of Inadon 1: The Disc (Co-written with Storm and Rhys Petersen) (short story in Game On! Anthology)

Post Apocalyptic Sci-Fi

Compulsive Directive

NONFICTION

A Year Of Weekly Writing Exercises (Creative Writing)

Cooking For Families With Allergies (Cooking) (Co-written with Storm Petersen)

Tell Me A Story, Grandma (Memoir)

For the most up to date details on available titles visit:

www.avrilsabine.com/books/bibliography

Disclaimer

This is a work of fiction. Names, characters, businesses, places, events and incidents are either the products of the author's imagination or used in a fictitious manner. Any resemblance to actual persons, living or dead, or actual events is purely coincidental. The opinions expressed or beliefs held are those of the characters and should not be assumed to be the opinions or beliefs of the author.

www.ingramcontent.com/pod-product-compliance
Lightning Source LLC
Chambersburg PA
CBHW050808190726
48285CB00005B/1837